TOWN TAMER

Tom Rosser was a lawman without a town and a gunfighter with a mission — to shoot down the bushwhackers who had killed his sweetheart. Great Plains was the last and most lawless boomtown, a town that needed a man like Rosser. Riley Condor was the bait to get Rosser to Great Plains, for he was the very man Rosser had sworn to kill. Before long there would be a bloody showdown no one would ever forget.

Books by Frank Gruber
in the Linford Western Library:

TALES OF WELLS FARGO
BROKEN LANCE
GUNSIGHT
THE MARSHAL
RIDE TO HELL
BITTER SAGE
FIGHTING MAN

FRANK GRUBER

TOWN TAMER

Complete and Unabridged

LINFORD
Leicester

First published in the
United States of America

First Linford Edition
published June 1992

British Library CIP Data

Gruber, Frank
    Town tamer.—Large print ed.—
Linford western library
I. Title II. Series
823.912 [F]

ISBN 0–7089–7179–2

Published by
F. A. Thorpe (Publishing) Ltd.
Anstey, Leicestershire
Set by Words & Graphics Ltd.
Anstey, Leicestershire
Printed and bound in Great Britain by
T. J. Press (Padstow) Ltd., Padstow, Cornwall

1

LEE RING tied his horse to a pole behind Riley Condor's Kansas Saloon, rolled a cigarette and lighted it, while his eyes searched the alley to the right and left. Then, satisfied, he moved swiftly to a door and knocked on it.

The door was opened after a moment by Riley Condor himself. Condor's right hand was in the pocket of his sack coat, gripping a short-barreled .41 derringer. He looked inquiringly at Ring.

"Mr. Condor?" Ring asked carefully.

Condor shrugged. "Who're you?"

"I got a letter from Mr. Condor. You write it?"

"That depends. What's your name?"

Ring hesitated. "This letter came to me, in Idaho . . . "

Condor took his hand out of his

coat pocket and pulled the door open wider. "You're cautious enough to be Lee Ring."

Ring bobbed his head and stepped into Condor's office, which was at the rear of his saloon. Condor closed the door leading to the alley and bolted it.

"You've got the letter with you?"

"No," said the man from Idaho, "but I can tell you what was in it. It asked if I was interested in earning two thousand dollars."

"What would you expect to do for two thousand?"

"You tell me, Mr. Condor."

"Would you kill a man?"

"You don't get two thousand for digging a row of potatoes."

"That's right, Ring. And for that matter you don't usually get two thousand for killing a man, do you?"

Ring made a gesture of dismissal. "You set the price, Mr. Condor."

"Not exactly. I'm not in this alone. Ten of the businessmen of this town put up two hundred dollars each. There's a man we want — ah — eliminated."

"It's none of my business, Mr. Condor," Ring said slowly, "but if the businessmen are behind this, couldn't you get your marshal to chase this man out of town?"

"The man happens to be the marshal."

"Tom Rosser?"

"You've heard of him?"

Lee Ring pinched out the butt of his cigarette and carried it to an ash tray where he deposited it carefully. Then he said, "Yes, I've heard of Tom Rosser."

"You can handle him?"

"Like you said, two thousand is a lot of money."

"Rosser's a lot of man."

There was always a hush in the early evening, after the businessmen closed their stores and went to their homes, when the workingmen left their jobs and had their suppers and before they left their homes again for the saloons.

Tom Rosser had never liked the quiet of the early evening. It always seemed to him that it was the lull before the storm, the time when the men who opposed him were laying their plans for the evening, when the saloonkeepers were watering their whiskey, the gamblers rigging their games and the men with the guns cleaning the tools of their trade.

He stood on the wooden sidewalk in front of Eli's Emporium and watched the batwing doors of Riley Condor's Kansas Saloon across the street. There were ten saloons in Broken Lance and the owners of all of them hated Tom Rosser, but Riley Condor owned the biggest saloon in town and his hatred for Tom Rosser was proportionately greater.

Grady Parish, Rosser's deputy, came up as he stood outside Eli's Emporium.

"Goin' to be a little nippy tonight," Parish observed.

"It's October."

"Fella visitin' Condor," Parish said

quietly. "Saw his horse at Doc Meany's stable. The brand's an Idaho one."

"Idaho?"

"Thought you might have missed it."

Rosser took out a thin, twisted stogie and bit off an end. He stuffed the cigar in his mouth, but did not light it.

His eyes went to the veranda of the Kansas Hotel. Carol Grannan had come out. She wore a dark green dress and Rosser knew that she had seen him and was waiting for him to come to the hotel and have supper with her.

A stranger with an Idaho horse. It was a small thing, but Rosser was still alive because he never overlooked the little things, the seemingly insignificant.

He nodded carelessly to the deputy and crossed the street. He kept his eyes from going in the direction of the hotel as he headed for the Kansas Saloon.

He entered. There were only a few customers this early. A small poker game was going on and two regulars were leaning against the bar. One of

5

the bartenders was polishing glasses and the other was pouring out a glass of whiskey for one of the customers at the bar.

The bartender, pouring out the whiskey, saw Rosser and shot a quick glance at the closed door of Riley Condor's private office.

"Evenin', Mr. Rosser."

Rosser did not even look at the bartender. He continued on to the rear and the first bartender signaled frantically to the man polishing the glasses, who was at the far end of the bar.

The man came quickly around the bar. "Mr. Condor's havin' his supper," he said loudly.

Rosser made a flickering gesture with his left hand and the bartender moved aside. He might lose his job for it, but no man in Broken Lance stood in Tom Rosser's path. However, the bartender's loud announcement had been heard inside Condor's office, and when Rosser tried to push open the door, he found it locked.

"Yes?" Condor's voice asked, from inside the office.

"Rosser!"

"Just a minute." There was a moment's pause, then the bolt was released and Riley Condor pulled open the door. He stepped back and Rosser swung the door in, hard, so that it slammed back against the wall and assured him that no one was hiding behind it.

There was no one inside the room except Condor, but there were no supper dishes in the room either, which Rosser noted.

"Where's your visitor?" Rosser asked, looking at the alley door.

"Visitor?" Condor made a mocking gesture about the room.

"Man from Idaho."

Condor grunted. "You're so damn spooked you're seeing killers behind every door."

"There's a horse at Doc Meany's stable with an Idaho brand . . . "

7

"Rosser," Condor said, coldly savage, "you've been throwing your weight around, like you were a marshal, judge and executioner, all rolled into one. I'm fed up with you and so are a helluva lot of people around here . . ."

"That's why you've sent for the Idaho man?"

Condor became suddenly cold sober. "I haven't sent anywhere for anyone, but it may not be a bad idea, Rosser. It may not be a bad idea at all."

"I've said my piece, Condor. Tell your friend from Idaho that I know he's here."

Rosser turned abruptly and walked out of the office.

2

OUTSIDE the Kansas Saloon, Rosser stood for a moment, uncertainly. Carol Grannan was still on the veranda of the hotel. She would wait and even if he did not show up, she would not say anything about it. Yet it would be between them and the question would be in her eyes, if not on her lips.

He went toward the hotel, and as his eyes took in Carol, a glow of warmth spread through him. She was a handsome woman, reaching twenty-five, and she should have been married and living in a home of her own. She should have had two children by now. Instead, she clerked at Eaton's Dry Goods Store in Broken Lance.

She had a slender, yet mature figure. Her eyes were a greyish blue and her features were finely chiseled. Her hair was a deep auburn, almost mahogany.

She said, as Rosser climbed the stairs to the hotel veranda, "I was just waiting for a man to come along and buy me my dinner."

"The drummers quit coming to town?"

"The drummers want to sell me corsets and dresses, shoes and pinafores. When I eat with a man I want him to look at me as if I was a woman, not a prospective buyer of Danton's French Corsets and Bowy's Ladies' Shoes with elastic tops."

They went into the hotel dining room and a waitress began to bring them food. They did not have to order for this was Tuesday, and on Tuesday the main course was underdone roast beef, just as it was overdone steak on Wednesday.

They were eating the soggy dried-apple pie when Carol said quietly, "What is it, Tom?"

"Eh?"

"Your mind's elsewhere."

"I'm sorry." He tried a smile, but dropped his eyes from her steady look.

"You've told the town council that you're leaving Saturday?"

"I thought I'd tell them tomorrow."

"You are quitting Saturday?"

"Yes. I think so."

"You *think* so?"

Rosser said defensively, "The end of the season, I said."

"Saturday's the last day of the month," Carol declared, "and as for the season, it's already over. No herd has reached Broken Lance in ten days. There won't be another." A spot of color appeared in her cheeks. "You said you'd have enough of wearing a badge . . ."

"I have, Carol. I never wanted to be a marshal in the first place and it's been on my mind that this was my last year — "

"Then why delay telling the town council that you're through?"

Rosser hesitated. "As a matter of fact, I told Mayor Horton a month ago that I'd be quitting at the end of the season. Only now . . . something's come up . . . there's a man here from Idaho . . . "

Carol exclaimed poignantly, "One more man you've got to fight? One more man you've got to kill . . . "

"This one's been brought in by Riley Condor . . . "

"You said you wanted to be a rancher," Carol went on, heedless. "You — you talked about the life we would have when you stopped being a target for every man in the West . . . "

"We'll have that life," Rosser said earnestly. He saw the storm come into her eyes and added quickly, "I can't run out on a fight, Carol. I can't quit under fire . . . "

"*I* can," she flashed. "I'm taking the eastbound, Saturday with you . . . " She paused, then added, "or without you."

Rosser said, "Don't make it an ultimatum."

12

"Maybe I should have made it that a year ago. Two years ago." Then she exclaimed poignantly, "Turn in your badge. Tonight . . . "

A frown creased his forehead. "I can't, tonight. Perhaps tomorrow, or the day after."

"Or next week? Maybe the week after?" Despair came into her voice. "It's now, Tom. Or never!"

"Don't press me. I'll try to go with you Saturday."

"If you're alive by then!" She suddenly pushed back her chair. "I mean it, Tom. I'm going Saturday."

She got to her feet.

"Wait, Carol!"

She waited. He saw the stiffness in her body and he could not talk to her. He had seldom been able to talk to her. He did not have the words.

She waited and after a moment he made a helpless gesture and she walked out of the dining room. Rosser paid the bill and strolled out. He stood in the lobby for a moment or two, but she

13

had apparently gone to her room.

He crossed to the mud-chinked log building that was a combination marshal's office and jail. Grady Parish sat at a small desk, inside the room, staring gloomily at a rack containing two shotguns and a Winchester.

"You were right about Condor," Rosser said. "He's brought in a man, all right, but he doesn't want me to see him." He paused. "I guess it isn't going to be a stand-up fight."

A fine film of perspiration showed on Parish's face, although the air had grown cold with the setting of the sun.

"I'll back you, Tom."

"You're a married man and it isn't your fight."

"Is it yours?"

"You know it is. I'm the one Condor's after."

Parish said worriedly, "I've caught a whisper or two around town. It isn't just Condor. They're all in it. They've made up a purse for — for the gunfighter."

"That figures. But Condor's still their leader. The Idaho man's with *him*."

A boy of sixteen or seventeen came into the marshal's office. "Mr. Rosser," he said, "I've got a message for you."

"All right, let's see it."

"It isn't a note. She told me to tell you — Miss Carol . . . "

"Yes?"

"She wants to talk to you."

"Where?"

"At the hotel."

Rosser hesitated, then took a half dollar from his pocket. The boy backed away. "No, Miss Carol already gave me a half dollar."

"All right, thanks. You've delivered the message."

The boy turned and ran out of the office. Rosser looked at the door but did not move toward it and Parish suddenly exclaimed and pushed back his chair.

"Tom, you don't think — ?"

"No," Rosser said quickly. "I just

had dinner with Carol and — we had words."

Parish relaxed. "I see."

Rosser went out of the office, but instead of crossing the street and going to the hotel, he turned left and walked to the livery stable a half block away.

In the years he had known her, Carol Grannan had never sent him a message. It wasn't in her nature to do so. Any word she had to get to him, she would deliver herself.

The night hostler was in charge of the stable, a whiskey-soaked oldster, who could not hold down a regular job. He sat in a tilted chair, his eyes rheumy and his coat pocket sagging from the weight of a bottle.

"Ambrose," Rosser said, "you've got an Idaho horse here."

"We got buckskin horses, we got paint horses and we got roans, but how would the likes of me know whether a horse is from Idaho or Dakota?"

"The brand," said Rosser. "Anyway, the man who rode the horse brought

16

him in this afternoon."

"I got a dun here, with a Walking W brand. Could be Idaho, but Doc Meany put him up. I wouldn't know the owner if I saw him." He suddenly scowled. "That why Doc went huntin' this afternoon?"

"Perhaps, although I never knew Doc to be a friend to Riley Condor."

Rosser shook his head and left the stable. On the street he stood for a moment looking at the hotel, then drew a deep breath and walked down the street. Crossing, he entered the Kansas Saloon. Even before he entered he was aware of the unusual stillness inside. It was late enough for the place to be enjoying its full evening play.

The same small poker game was still going on and a half-dozen men stood around a faro game, but there were only three or four customers at the bar. The door of Riley Condor's office stood open. There was no one inside.

Rosser knew that eyes were watching him furtively as he left the saloon.

Outside he reached down and slid his Navy Colt in and out of its smooth holster, just to make sure that it was not stuck.

He walked slowly along the wooden sidewalk, darting glances ahead, to both sides of him. There was a wide, dark space between the Bon Ton Millinery Shop and Flugel's Photographic Studio, and as he came up to it, his hand went down and touched the cold butt of his revolver.

Nothing happened, however, and he continued on to the hotel.

The lobby was deserted, the night clerk having left his post. Rosser stepped to the door of the dining room. The clerk and a late customer were eating inside, but the waitresses were already cleaning up.

Rosser returned to the desk. Key #6 was gone from the key rack. That was as it should be. He looked for a long moment at the stairs leading to the second floor, then finally went to them and began climbing.

On the second floor, he looked down a hall lighted only by a dim lantern, hung on the wall halfway down the corridor. The far end was in heavy gloom. There were six doors on each side.

All the doors were closed.

He started down the hall, walking slowly, making no attempt to soften his footsteps. But his ears were attuned as they had never been in his life. The slightest movement inside a room, the faintest squeak of a door opening . . .

He reached the door of Number 6, listened, then knocked lightly.

"Yes?" It was her voice inside the room.

"Tom."

He could hear the quick inhaling of her breath, then her footsteps as she came quickly to the door. She opened it and looked up at him, her eyes wide.

"Come in," she said poignantly. Although he had never been in her room and there had never been the slightest hint of such things between them, she opened the door for him now without the least hesitation.

He did not enter, however. "Did you send a message?"

"A mes . . . " She never finished the question.

Her eyes looked beyond Rosser and widened in shock. Behind Rosser, the door of Room Number 4 had opened noiselessly on well-oiled hinges. The muzzle of a gun was thrust out. Thunder rocked the narrow hallway of the hotel. The bullet snuffed out the lamp on the wall, plunging the hall into darkness, save for the shaft of light from the open door of Carol's room.

Rosser was reaching for his gun and whirling when the other man's gun roared. He threw himself forward and sideward when the gun thundered for the second time. Wind tugged at him as the bullet missed him narrowly. Then Rosser was firing.

He fired once as he was going down,

a second time after he hit the floor and then, a third time, as boots pounded the floor boards.

He had no target at which to shoot, was firing blindly and his quarry was fleeing; Rosser knew that. He scrambled to his feet, coiled to pursue . . . when a strangled sob stopped him. He turned and in the light from Carol's room saw her huddled body on the floor.

The shock staggered him. He sprang back and fell to his knees beside her.

"Carol!" he cried out in horror.

She was lying partly on her side. Bloody froth was already welling up from her mouth, but her eyes were still open.

They met Rosser's and he saw for an instant the anguish in them. Then life went out of the eyes.

Rosser's hands, reaching for her, froze in mid-air. For a long moment he knelt on the floor, staring down at what remained of Carol Grannan. Then the sound of a door slamming downstairs sent a shudder through his body. He got to his feet.

"Goodbye, my dear," he said softly.

Rosser strode into the Kansas Saloon. The door of Riley Condor's office stood open. He went to it, looked into the empty room and turned to find the eyes of both bartenders on him.

"Riley had some business in Kansas City," one of the bartenders said. "He took the six forty eastbound."

3

IN the afternoons Rosser sat at the corner table in the hotel saloon and had two glasses of whiskey. He was oblivious to the activity around him and sat slouched back in his chair, his eyes on the whiskey and the table. He generally spent an hour with the two whiskies.

He had been doing this every day for more than two weeks, when a man approached his table one afternoon, shortly after Rosser's second whiskey had been placed before him. He was a well-built man of about forty-five, wearing a conservative business suit, a ruffled white shirt and a black cravat.

"Do you mind if I sit down, Mr. Rosser?" he asked.

Rosser raised his eyes from the whiskey. "I don't own the place."

The stranger seated himself and

extended a card to Rosser. The latter, annoyed, tried to ignore the card but the hand that held it remained steady.

Rosser finally took the card and glancing at it, read: 'James Fenimore Fell.'

"You've heard of me?"

"A man named Fell is building the Minnesota & Pacific."

"I am that man." Fell drew in a deep breath and exhaled. "Mr. Rosser, I paid the Pinkerton Detective Agency a thousand dollars for a report on you."

Rosser was finally roused from his lethargy. "Eh?"

"You've done a considerable amount of traveling since last October. You've been to Virginia City, Nevada, to San Francisco — New Orleans . . . "

"And two weeks ago I came to St. Paul," Rosser said coolly. "Your detective agency told you that."

"That's right." Fell took a folded document from his breast pocket. "In the Pinkerton report it said that you talked to people about becoming a rancher, someday. Well, this is a deed to that ranch. The nucleus of it, at any rate. Six hundred and forty acres of land in Montana. A present from the Minnesota & Pacific Railroad."

Rosser regarded Fell sharply. "Why should you give me a section of land?"

"Because of a proposition I am going to make you. You know that I am building a railroad, but you do not know *how* I am building that railroad."

"Is there more than one way?"

Fell did not seem to hear Rosser's question. He continued, "I'm building the Minnesota & Pacific out of earnings. We lay a hundred miles of track, then bring in colonists; farmers for the land, businessmen for the towns. From the freight and passenger revenue — and the sale of land — we build another hundred miles of track. Our first year we built to Fargo, our second to Bismarck, the third to Williston and last fall to Wolf Point. This year — this year of 1886 — we're risking everything. We're going to lay two hundred miles of track to Great Plains, a townsite we've laid out, which is going to be the biggest city between St. Paul and the Pacific Coast. We've risked everything, my associates and I. All this past winter, we've conducted an advertising campaign that has brought us the largest number of land and townsite applications we've ever had. These people are going into eastern and central Montana, into the richest land our railroad has yet tapped, soil that will grow any kind of crop, grazing land for sheep and cattle and mines that are richer than the mines of Nevada. If we can lay our two hundred miles of track this year — and hold it — the Minnesota & Pacific will be a success. In three years we'll reach the Pacific."

"Good," said Rosser carelessly. "I hope you make it."

"We've *got* to make it," Fell said earnestly. "This land deed is for a section near Great Plains. As it stands now the land isn't worth more than fifty cents an acre, certainly no more than a dollar. But if the railroad reaches Great Plains, your section will have a substantial value."

"I haven't accepted it," Rosser said, annoyed. "I know you're getting at something, but . . . what?"

"Every railhead we've had," Fell went on, "has become a boom town. Every town has attracted the scum of the West, gamblers, saloonkeepers, thieves, killers. We need a steady stream of immigrants. We need them this year more than we ever needed them. Reports of lawlessness, violence, cannot trickle back and frighten away the immigrants. Great Plains must therefore be kept under control. We cannot have the lawlessness of our previous towns. We cannot take the chance. We're gambling too much . . . "

"Well, you finally got to it," Rosser said grimly. "You're offering me the job of marshal of Great Plains?"

Fell shook his head. "No. That's one thing we cannot do — interfere with the local governments. We sell land to settlers, town lots to business people, but we cannot govern them. That's up to the people themselves. They must form their own governments, elect their own officials. Of course we can *help* them, but that help has to be unofficial."

"Are you suggesting that I go to this — this Great Plains, and *run* for office?"

"Not exactly. Even if you were elected, your responsibility would be to the people. There might be times when their interests would be adverse to those of the railroad." Fell shook his head. "I'll put it to you bluntly. I want you to go the Great Plains, as my personal representative."

"And?"

"See that the town is kept under control."

"In other words, you want me to be the town tamer?"

"Yes. You will have no official status. You will *not* be working for the railroad, although you will have the railroad's

28

interests in mind, at all times."

"What you mean," said Rosser, "is that if I get in trouble, the railroad doesn't back me?"

"That's about the size of it. You'll be on your own. You will work with the authorities, if that is possible, if not, you will work without them. Your duties will be — "

"To tame the town!"

"Yes!"

"And my pay is this section of land?"

"No. That is a gift. It's yours simply because — well — because I think it would be good for you to have a personal stake in the country. But, for the time you are in Great Plains, you will be paid."

"A regular salary, or so much for every man I kill?"

Fell winced. "You speak bluntly, Mr. Rosser."

"You're talking bluntly yourself."

"Of course. Forgive me. You will be paid a salary. Shall we say — three hundred dollars a month?"

"I got only a hundred a month at Broken Lance."

"I know that. This work will be — ah — more strenuous."

Rosser nodded. slowly. "The pay is good, Mr. Fell, but . . . I'm not going to take the job."

Fell exclaimed in chagrin. "Why not?"

"Because I've got some personal business to take care of."

Fell stared at Rosser, then suddenly his eyes lit up.

"The Pinkerton report . . . it told about your last days in Broken Lance. The unfortunate death of — of the woman, who — "

The sudden coldness of Rosser's eyes stopped Fell. But only for a moment. He exclaimed softly, "That was six months ago, Rosser! You can't spend the rest of your life seeking revenge."

Rosser said icily, "We have nothing further to discuss, Mr. Fell."

Fell looked at Rosser for a long

moment, then got heavily to his feet and without another word left the saloon.

Minutes later a waiter came to Rosser's table. "That will be all, sir?" he asked.

Rosser indicated the glass. "No, I'll have another."

It was the first time he had ordered a third drink. He drank it slowly and then got up and went into the hotel lobby. He sat down in a great armchair, near the door and stared out upon the activity of the spring-muddy street of St. Paul.

4

A WOMAN entered the hotel and went to the desk. After a few moments she returned and began to pace back and forth.

Rosser, diverted by the nervous pacing, finally looked at the woman. He had seen her before, for she seemed to spend much time in the hotel lobby.

She was quite young, he noticed now, not more than twenty-two. She was fairly tall, slender, yet willowy. Her hair was reddish brown, almost mahogany. Her features were regular, and she was probably a very attractive young woman when her face bore less strain than it did now.

As he watched her, Rosser saw that her eyes went to the door of the hotel saloon and he recalled now that he had observed her once or twice, briefly, with a man who spent much time in the perpetual card game in the hotel saloon, a dark-haired, olive-skinned man, a flashy dresser, with a diamond ring and a pearl stickpin in his cravat. A professional gambler.

Even as the mental description flitted through his mind, the man came out of the saloon. The woman saw him and went to him. Rosser heard the sharp voice of the man, the low, pleading tone of the woman, then saw them both leave the hotel, the man a step ahead, the woman walking swiftly to keep up with him.

A little later Rosser drifted to the desk and lighting a cigar, observed to the clerk, "The dark fellow who came out of the bar a few minutes ago . . . sporting man, isn't he?"

The clerk closed one eye. "Mr. Guy Tavenner. I guess you might call him a sporting man. Cards, good whiskey, plenty of it, and — mmm — that wife of his, who's always waiting around for him. You ask me, a woman with her looks . . . "

Rosser turned away from the desk and walked out of the lobby. On the veranda, he seated himself in a cane-bottomed chair.

And then, in a blinding flash, it came to him!

The woman reminded him of Carol Grannan, the memory of whom he had tried so hard to forget these last few months, the memory of whom . . .

Angrily, Rosser got up, stepped down from the veranda and took a swift walk up the street. He walked until he was tired, then turned and went back to the hotel. Yet he could not go to his room. He knew that he would lie on the bed, sleepless, and stare at the ceiling and see her face. There had been too many such days, such nights.

He went into the hotel saloon, ordered a drink at the bar and tossed it down and poured out a second glass.

A poker game was going on at one of the tables and Rosser, after a few minutes, strolled to the game. The house player, who wore an eyeshade and sleeve guards, looked at him smilingly.

"We can use a sixth player."

Rosser pulled out a chair, seated himself and took three double eagles from his pocket. The players regarded the gold with approval.

A hand was played which Rosser won with a pair of kings. Then Guy Tavenner came into the bar, his dark face scowling. He came to the poker game.

"I see we've got fresh money," he observed, smirking at Rosser.

One of the players dealt. It was draw poker and since no one had openers, the deal was passed along. One of the players opened the second game and Tavenner stayed and raised the opening bet by five dollars. Rosser dropped out and Tavenner gave him an open sneer. Tavenner won the pot finally, but there was less than forty dollars in it.

It was Rosser's deal, then. When Tavenner opened for twenty dollars, Rosser dropped out. One man only remained and Tavenner again won, another small pot.

Rosser stayed in the next game, but did not win, one of the others players winning, against two raises by Tavenner. It was Tavenner's turn to deal then and he passed out the cards with a flourish. The first man opened for five dollars. Rosser stayed, but when it came Tavenner's turn, the dealer raised the bet ten dollars. Surprisingly, four players, including Rosser, called the raise.

The opener drew one card and checked. The next man looked at his three-card draw and tossed in his hand, as did another player. Rosser drew two cards and without looking at them tossed a five-dollar bill into the pot. Tavenner drew two cards, putting them carefully face down. He called Rosser's bet and raised it ten dollars.

The opening player frowned worriedly, but finally put out fifteen dollars. Rosser, still without looking at his cards, called Tavenner's ten-dollar raise and hiked it ten.

Tavenner looked at his hand, hesitated and then called the ten and raised it twenty. "I've seen *my* hand," he said, thinly.

The man who had opened, squeezed out his cards once more, started to count out money, then suddenly changed his mind and threw in his hand. The game was now between Tavenner and Rosser and the latter had not yet looked at his two-card draw, but without hesitation he called Tavenner's twenty-dollar raise and reaching into his pocket brought out his last double eagle. He tossed it into the pot.

Tavenner exclaimed angrily, "What kind of playing do you call that? Look at your cards."

"I prefer not to."

"I went in with three jacks," Tavenner snapped.

"I had three queens," Rosser said quietly.

"Yeah? Well, *I* picked up a pair of sixes."

"In which case you'll beat me . . . if I didn't add to the queens."

Tavenner scowled savagely, looked again at his hand and drummed his fingers on the tabletop. He counted out his money, found that he had only fourteen dollars. "I'm going to call and raise you fifty," he finally said.

"Put it on the table."

"I've only got fourteen dollars here. The rest is in my room . . . "

"I'll wait until you get it."

"Damn it," swore Tavenner, "I thought this was a gentleman's game."

One of the other play put in a word: "This game is table stakes. You can call for fourteen dollars, Mr. Tavenner. If you haven't got the money on you, you can't raise."

Tavenner gave the man an angry look and shoved in his money. He flipped over his cards. "Beat the full house."

Rosser turned over his original three

cards, revealing three queens. He turned over one of the two draw cards, a deuce. The triumph grew on Tavenner's face and then Rosser turned up the last card. A queen.

Tavenner let out a roar of anguish. "Fool's luck!"

Rosser began gathering up his money. He pushed back his chair. "Deal me out."

"You can't quit now," snarled Tavenner. "Not when I'm behind."

"It seems to me you're broke," Rosser said evenly.

"My I.O.U.'s good."

"Is it?"

Tavenner pointed at one of the players. "You'll cash a check for me?"

"No," was the blunt reply.

Tavenner bared his teeth, was about to make a devastating accusation, then suddenly became crafty. He fixed Rosser with a glittering look. "You're the winner. You can cash a check for me."

"No," said Rosser. "I have an

arrangement with the bank. They don't play poker and I don't cash checks."

"Damn you for a piker," swore Tavenner.

Taut-lipped, Rosser walked away from the table. He stopped at the bar, had a drink, then walked out of the saloon. The poker game resumed, without Tavenner, who watched the game for a minute or two, then went to the bar.

Rosser went into the lobby, where he bought a cigar and the St. Paul newspaper. He sat down in a chair near the window and read the paper. He was almost through when Mrs. Tavenner came into the hotel from the street. He watched her go to the desk, get her key, then climb the stairs to the second floor.

Rosser reread a page or two of the newspaper and was putting it aside when Susan Tavenner came down the stairs. She started for the door, but when she reached it, she turned aside and stood for a moment, looking toward the door of the hotel saloon.

Guy Tavenner, his dark face flushed, came out of the bar. He saw his wife and bore down on her.

"Why didn't you come in and drag me out?" he sneered.

"Please!" Mrs. Tavenner said in a low, anguished tone. "Don't make a scene."

"Then stop following me around," snapped Tavenner, "I'm getting fed up with your snooping and nagging."

"Guy!" exclaimed Susan Tavenner.

The palm of Guy Tavenner's hand caught her squarely on the left cheek. It was a resounding crack, that could have been heard even in the saloon, from which Tavenner had just come.

"Damn you for a sniveling female," Tavenner raged.

Rosser, who had never, even in his wildest thoughts, seen himself interfering in a domestic quarrel between a husband and wife, suddenly found himself on his feet, striding toward Guy

41

Tavenner and his wife.

But Susan Tavenner herself stopped Rosser. She saw him coming, her face tear-stained, livid from her husband's blow. Rushing toward Rosser — and past him — she cried in low anguish, "Don't . . . don't interfere!"

She continued on, out of the hotel. Guy Tavenner, who had guessed Rosser's intent, came toward him. "You want what I just gave her?" he demanded savagely.

Rosser made, then, one of the hardest decisions he ever had been called upon to make. He turned away from Tavenner.

Tavenner's taunting laugh followed him as he climbed the steps to his room on the second floor.

In his room, Rosser took off his coat and threw himself on the bed. As he thought of Tavenner, a slow anger grew in him. What kind of a man would slap his wife in the lobby of a hotel? And what kind of a woman was she that she would take it?

A woman who reminded Rosser of . . .

A shudder ran through him. Exclaiming, he raised himself and swung his feet to the floor. He got his coat and put it on. He went down the stairs, to the hotel lobby, through it to the cooling night air.

Again he walked long blocks. He reached the banks of the Mississippi and stood in the darkness, staring at the shimmering lights that were the village of St. Anthony, on the other side.

West and south was Kansas, where Carol Grannan was buried in a lonely grave, in a country that she had never really liked, where she had remained only because of Tom Rosser . . . where she had died because of Rosser.

The Tavenners occupied the most expensive suite in the hotel, an elaborately furnished sitting room with a connecting bedroom, which contained a four-poster bed. That he had never paid a dollar of the rent did not worry Guy Tavenner. He was used to such things, just as he was accustomed to throwing money about in regal fashion, when he had it. Which was not too often.

He was pacing the carpeted floor of the sitting room, when Susan Tavenner entered, after the longest walk she had ever taken in a dark, strange city.

Tavenner exclaimed hotly when he saw his wife. "Where have you been?"

Susan said, "You will never touch me again."

"I haven't got time to argue," Tavenner snapped. "I've had the devil's own luck. I need some money."

"I have no more money to give you."

"Fifty dollars will see me through."

"I haven't got fifty dollars."

"I'll give it back to you. I've already sent a wire to my partner in Great Plains. He's sending me five hundred. Enough to pay all our bills and to get us there."

44

Susan shook her head. "I'm sorry, Guy. I can't give it to you. I couldn't if I wanted to and I don't — "

Guy Tavenner strode toward Susan. The latter, half expecting him to strike her again, threw up her hands. One held her handbag and Tavenner snatched it from her. He whisked it open, plunged a hand inside and brought out several feminine articles that he threw aside. He came upon a thin packet of bills and began to count them.

"Twenty, thirty, thirty-five, thirty-eight dollars . . . this is all you've got?"

"All I have left of the five hundred," cried Susan. "You — you can't take it from me . . . you can't!"

Tavenner thrust the money into his pocket and tossed her handbag to a nearby chair. "Don't wait up for me."

"Guy!"

Tavenner whipped open the door and went out.

A sob wracked Susan Tavenner and

she stumbled to the chair where he had flung her purse.

This was the end. She had seen it coming for the past several days, had fought against it, but she knew now that she could go on no longer. The last few dollars he had taken from her did not matter. She had already reconciled herself to losing all of the money with which she had left home six weeks ago.

It was the deterioration of her relationship with Guy that had come to the cataclysmic finale. Seven weeks ago she had not even known him. She had lived a quiet life in the little Indiana town. She had attended her church on Sundays and the Welfare Meetings on Wednesday evenings. She had her circle of friends, whom she visited and who visited her. She had her parents.

She even had a suitor. Lester Cahill, a balding man, just under thirty, who worked in the bank. Eventually he would become cashier of the bank. Even now, he was a respected member of the community. Not exciting, but well regarded by everyone.

They had never become formally engaged, although there was talk of marriage. Lester paid regular attendance upon her and it was taken for granted among their friends that Susan would become Mrs. Cahill. In her own mind, Susan had not resisted the idea.

Not until Guy Tavenner appeared in the village. She had seen him sitting on the veranda of the hotel one evening, as she passed with Lester on the way to the Wednesday-night meeting at the church. On the way home the swarthy stranger was still on the hotel veranda and the following day he had accosted her on the street.

She should have ignored him, of course, but he was extraordinarily handsome . . . and he was courtesy itself. He knew her name and said that he had called upon her father at the store, that morning.

He was a drummer, he said.

She knew about drummers. She had

been told about them ever since she had pinned up her pigtails. A girl did not talk to drummers.

Guy Tavenner was not easily discouraged. He had to stay in town two days more, to await some important orders from his home office, in Chicago. He had no further business in town and time weighed heavily. The countryside was beautiful and he suggested a drive in the country.

She refused, but he appeared at her house within the hour in a rented buggy. She went with him.

The next day she drew her five hundred dollars from the bank and took the train to Chicago. With Guy Tavenner.

They were married in Chicago. They lived at the Palmer House, which was reputed to have a barbership that had a floor inlaid with silver dollars. They ate in fine restaurants and had a wonderful time. Tavenner was handsome and he was charming. Susan missed him in the evenings, when he had his business conferences. They had been married three weeks before Susan learned the nature of her husband's business. They left the hotel late at night and in the hansom that took them to the railroad depot, Tavenner borrowed a hundred dollars from her, which he promised to repay in St. Louis.

In St. Louis they checked into the Planters Hotel and lived handsomely for two weeks, when they again left the hotel at night and boarded a boat that eventually brought them to St. Paul. Susan again gave her husband money to pay their passage.

They were going to Montana, Tavenner told her. He had met a man in St. Louis with whom he was going into business. A new country, a new run of luck.

Susan was already disillusioned when they arrived in St. Paul, but there was nothing else she could do. She had burned her bridges behind her.

Home?

She had written to her father and

mother from Chicago. They were living in a magnificent hotel and would soon move into their own home. Guy was a man of substance. He was known to many important people. In the restaurants they called him by his name.

All of those things Susan wrote to her parents, because Guy had told them to her. She could not tell them what she after learned. That they had been compelled to flee Chicago, because of her husband's gambling debts. She could not tell them that she was the wife of a professional gambler.

Not even now, when Tavenner had struck her, had forcibly taken her last dollar from her. She could not tell her family of that. She could not return to them.

She could never go home.

5

IT was the small hours of the morning before Rosser fell into a restless sleep. He slept late in the morning and it was after eight when he went downstairs and had breakfast in the dining room.

Finished, he strolled out to the lobby and saw Susan Tavenner at the desk. He was about to walk toward the street door when he heard her voice exclaim plaintively.

"My husband will take care of it," she was saying. "He'll give you the money as soon as he returns."

"Returns from where?" the manager asked coldly. "The maid tells me his luggage is gone, that he did not sleep in his bed last night."

"I know," said Susan Tavenner worriedly. "He — had to go to Montana. But he'll be back . . . "

"I am sorry, madam," the hotel manager said firmly. "I must have the money this morning. Two hundred dollars — and the amount of your bill, also."

"I haven't got it, Mr. Wagenheim," Susan Tavenner said. "I . . . Mr. Tavenner was short of cash and — "

"Mrs. Tavenner," the hotel manager said bluntly, "I am getting just a little tired of this fiction. Your husband gave me a bogus check for two hundred dollars and he's skipped. That's the truth of it, isn't it?"

"No, no!" cried Susan Tavenner desperately. "That — that's not so. My husband will return . . . "

"No one ever returns from Montana, ma'am," the hotel manager said firmly. "It's the jumping-off place to nowhere."

"He's going into business in Montana," Susan said hurriedly. "He had to go out and make some arrangements, then he's coming back for me . . . " She reached for her purse, fumbling as she tried to open it hastily. "Here — here's a letter from his partner. It — it proves what I said."

She thrust the letter at the hotel manager, who hesitated before taking it. He unfolded a sheet, glanced at it and shook his head.

"All this is, is a letter from someone named Condor, saying he will meet your husband at a place called Great Plains . . ."

"That's where they're opening a business. My husband and Mr. Riley Condor . . ."

Riley Condor.

Rosser listening, heard the name and a coldness seeped through his veins. He was only vaguely aware of the next words between the hotel manager and Susan Tavenner, but when she whirled away from the desk and hurried past him toward the door, his thoughts came back to the present.

He started to follow her, then swerved abruptly and seated himself in the armchair near the door.

He thought of Riley Condor. He

should have known. The cattle towns were playing out. The great trail herds of a few years ago were thinning down to a trickle. The railroads now reached into Texas. The boom towns at the end of the shifting Chisolm Trail . . . Ellsworth . . . Witchita . . . Dodge . . . Broken Lance . . . they had become quiet farming communities. Law had come to them, law and order.

The frontiers had receded. Only in the Northwest was there still virgin land. The railroads were now reaching into Dakota and Montana territories and opening them to civilization. They were creating new boom towns.

The vultures who fed and fattened in the boom towns of the West and Southwest were still alive. Like their feathered counterparts of the air they could see prey from great distances. If the Northwest was booming, that is where they would go.

What was it James Fenimore Fell had said to Rosser? Great Plains, in this year of 1886, would be the greatest of all the Western boom towns.

Riley Condor would be there.

There were no tears in Susan Tavenner's eyes when she left the St. Paul Hotel. She had shed them all during the small hours of the night while waiting for Guy Tavenner. The last had been only that mornïng when she had realized that he had deserted her.

She had left the hotel because there was nothing else to do. They would not permit her to return to her room. They would not allow her to take her luggage.

She had reached the end of the road. There was no way out of her dilemma. She was alone and destitute in a frontier town, five hundred miles from her home.

A man, perhaps, could exist in such circumstances. He could find work. He could, failing in that, beg for food. Or steal it. A woman . . . ?

A woman such as Susan Tavenner could only walk to the river bank

. . . and continue on.

Susan did, in fact, go toward the river, but before she reached it she saw, off to the right, the sprawling sheds of the railroad. Before she quite realized what she was doing, she was entering the depot and moving toward the ticket window.

"How — how much is a ticket to Chicago?" she managed to bring out, as the ticket clerk looked at her inquiringly.

"Twelve dollars and fifty cents." The man reached for a ticket but Susan hurriedly turned away from the window.

Twelve dollars and fifty cents. It might as well have been twelve hundred. She searched her bag and found in it eighty-five cents in silver that Tavenner had not thought worth taking.

She also found a gold band. Her wedding ring.

A shudder ran through her. Guy had sold his watch in St. Louis.

Susan left the depot, looked at the stores on the other side of the street.

One caught her eye. There were three gold-painted balls suspended over the doorway and lettering on the window read: North Star Loans.

She crossed the street, walked past the pawnshop, then returned and entered.

A whiskered old man was behind the counter.

"You have something to sell?" he asked wearily, noting Susan's agitation.

"Y-yes. My wedding ring."

He held out his hand. Susan dropped the ring into it. The pawnbroker gave it only a cursory glance. "I'm sorry, ma'am."

"You — you don't want it?"

"Madam," the old pawnbroker said quietly, "I buy and sell everything. Nothing is so trivial that someone, sometime, cannot find a use for it. I said that I was sorry merely because I assume that you believe this to be an expensive ring. It isn't."

"How much is it worth?"

"To you — I do not know. Perhaps

a great deal. To me it is brass, with a thin gold plating. I could not pay more than fifty cents."

Susan recoiled. The fleeting hope that had grown in her disappeared in a flash. There was nothing left for her but the river.

"Thank you," she said, "but fifty cents would not solve my problem."

"I am sorry." He held up his hand as Susan started to turn away. "The locket you are wearing. Perhaps . . . "

Susan stopped, hesitated, then turned back. She took the locket from about her throat. Her father and mother had given it to her on her eighteenth birthday.

The pawnbroker examined the locket. "This is very good," he said finally. "I can give you twenty dollars . . . " he hesitated. "Perhaps twenty-five."

A few minutes later, Susan returned to the railroad depot. The ticket seller recognized her. "One to Chicago?"

"No — I — I'd like to buy a ticket to Montana, Great Plains, Montana."

"Train doesn't go all the way. It will by the end of this year, but right now the best I can do is sell you a ticket to Wolf Point . . . fourteen dollars and twenty-five cents."

"How would I get from Wolf Point to Great Plains?"

"Stagecoach, ma'am."

"How much for the stage fare?"

"Ten dollars."

She could make it, with a dollar and sixty cents to spare. She bought the ticket to Wolf Point and an hour later boarded the train that was being prepared.

Rosser entered the pine-paneled office of James Fenimore Fell.

"If it isn't too late," he said, "I'd like to take that job in Great Plains."

Fell regarded Rosser thoughtfully for a moment. Then he nodded slowly. "I don't think I want to know the reason you changed your mind. The job is yours." He hesitated, then reached to a pile of papers at the side of his desk. He riffled through them and brought out a yellow sheet. "I received a telegram this morning from Great Plains. It seems that a group of public-spirited citizens decided to organize the town and county and have held an election. Would you like to know the results of that election?"

"No," said Rosser bluntly. "Every town I've ever been in has held elections. Sometimes the results have been good."

Fell glanced at the telegram. "Ever hear of a man named Wes Parker?"

"Don't believe I have."

"He's the new county sheriff. The man who owns a hotel is the Mayor of Great Plains . . . Joshua Moody. A lawyer named Murcott has been elected Judge. There are four city councilmen." Fell paused for a moment "Kenneth Rud, Harold Price, Fred Wagoner and — Riley Condor."

"Rud had a saloon in Wichita eight or nine years ago," Rosser said. "Price was a short-card man in Dodge City.

I don't know Fred Wagoner."

"It says here that he owns a saloon."

"I'm not surprised."

"Would the name of the Marshal of Great Plains surprise you? John Honsinger."

"It figures. They're going to make their last big cleanup."

"You still want the job?"

"Mr. Fell," Rosser said evenly, "we're both beating around the bush. You know I'm taking the job because I've learned that Riley Condor is in Great Plains."

Fell drummed his fingers on the desk. "The four councilmen are saloonkeepers and gamblers. The town marshal is a notorious gunfighter. I think I need you in Great Plains even more than I realized. When can you leave for Montana?"

"Tomorrow."

The train crossed the trestle that spanned the Mississippi and stopped for a few minutes at the busy little town of St. Anthony. Soon it was speeding along the flat countryside, past sparkling ponds of water that here and there were large enough to be called lakes. Farmsteads dotted the country, but soon gave way to heavy forests.

The train stopped for a half hour before dusk and the passengers streamed into a dining room that was part of the Fargo depot. For fifty cents, Susan Tavenner had her only meal of the day.

Some passengers had gotten off at Fargo, but there were new ones to take their places and the train, when it continued on into the night and the flat plains of the Dakota country, was full. There were immigrants on the train, men, women and children. Many of these people had not changed their clothing since leaving their former homes in Europe. The train reeked of unwashed humanity.

There was heavy breathing, snoring, the crying of children, through the night, the restless shifting about in the thinly cushioned seats. It was a long night and an uncomfortable one.

The following day was a bad one for Susan Tavenner. She breakfasted sparingly at a depot lunchroom and found, after paying, that she had only thirty-five cents left in her purse.

She ate no more that day and when she arrived at Wolf Point late that night, she remained in the newly constructed depot until morning, surrounded by immigrants who could not afford the hotels of the end-of-track town. But there was a difference. The immigrants had food.

The men went out into the town and returned with loaves of bread, sausages and other meats. They munched the food and watched their children wolf it. And Susan watched them.

In the morning she bought her ticket for the stagecoach and still kept her precious thirty-five cents in her purse.

The stagecoach stopped at a miserable relay station and the other passengers ate platefuls of messy-looking beans. Susan pleaded lack of appetite, but she was giddy by midafternoon. She slept in the coach that night, jolted about until her very bones were sore.

The stage driver pleaded with her to eat the following morning and when she refused, he bought her an apple. She pretended she was too ill to eat, but she ate every morsel of the apple, including the core. Later, she retched up most of it.

It was long after dark when the stagecoach finally rolled into Great Plains. Susan was barely able to walk into the hotel. Inside, she dropped into a chair and did not move until the hotel proprietor came to her.

"I — I am Mrs. Guy Tavenner," she said, summoning her last resources to make a brave front.

The hotel man could not restrain a soft whistle.

"You know Mr. Tavenner?" Susan asked eagerly.

The hotel man nodded without enthusiasm. "Checked in last night. He's at the Pleasure Palace."

"Where is it — this Pleasure Palace?"

"Down the street. But — you weren't thinking of going there?"

"Why not?"

Moody, the hotel man, frowned. "You're aware that it's a saloon and — and gambling hall?"

"Of course. My husband is a partner . . . "

"Partner? I thought he was one of the faro dealers."

"Faro is a — a gambling game?"

"Mrs. Tavenner," Moody said, "perhaps I'd better notify your husband that you are here. In the meantime, I suggest you — you go to his room."

Susan tried to rise, found that she had difficulty doing so and was grateful for the hotel man's helping arm. She swayed a little as he released her.

"The stagecoach trip was rather tiring."

"I'll show you upstairs."

Susan started to go with the hotel man, then suddenly stopped. "Did you say *room*?"

65

"Yes."

"I — I'm really quite tired. I wonder if it would be possible to have a room of my own?"

Moody regarded her steadily, then went behind the desk and consulted the key slots. He took down a key after a moment.

"Room seven," he said, as he came out from behind the desk. "It's next door to Tavenner's. But it does not have a connecting door."

"That's perfectly all right, Mr. — ?"

"Moody."

"Mr. Moody. And thank you."

It was an hour before Tavenner, without knocking, entered Susan's room. She was lying on the bed, fully dressed. Her right hand was clenched into a fist. He looked at her as she rose.

"So you followed me!"

"I couldn't go home."

"It would have been better for you if you had!"

"Perhaps," Susan said steadily, "but

when I married you — "

"Your mistake."

"Guy," Susan said poignantly, "I lost the last vestige of pride back in St. Paul. I've nothing left . . . nothing . . . "

"You apparently had some money," Tavenner sneered. "You didn't waste much time coming after me."

"I had no money, I — I sold the locket my father gave me."

Tavenner's eyes narrowed. "You've other jewelry?"

Susan opened the hand she had kept clenched. "Just this."

Tavenner still had the grace to flush a little. "Well, you're here." His eyes surveyed her appraisingly. "I must admit that I haven't seen anything better since leaving St. Paul."

His lips parted, he took a step toward her.

Susan retreated. "No!" she exclaimed softly.

"You're my wife," he said savagely, and caught her arm.

6

ROSSER got off the stagecoach in Great Plains and looked down the street of raw, unpainted buildings and wondered if this was the place where he would play out his last hand. The street was a long one, more than two blocks, and new buildings being erected at each end.

Yes, Great Plains would be a big place. The railroad was still months away, but already more than two hundred buildings were up, most of them business establishments, their owners waiting . . . waiting for the railroad and all that would come with the railroad. People . . . prosperity . . . perhaps death.

The driver of the stagecoach was unloading the luggage from the boot. He dropped Rosser's valise at his feet. Rosser picked it up, turned and saw the long, flat railroad depot some hundred yards away. Mountains of wooden crates, machinery, supplies and equipment of all sorts were piled about the building.

He turned back. His eyes picked out a two-story building of considerable size. A sign across the front read: MOUNTAIN HOTEL. Rosser walked to it and entered.

There was one room available, the clerk told Rosser. Three dollars a day. A bed with sheets cost a dollar extra. Rosser said he would do without sheets.

He carried his bag up to the room. It was about six feet wide and ten feet long. Two nails in the wall served in lieu of a closet. There was a narrow iron cot, a washstand with a pitcher and bowl; a single straight-backed chair.

The blankets on the bed were army blankets that had not been laundered too often.

Rosser unpacked his bag. He buckled his cartridge belt about his waist, tying the bottom of the holster about his thigh with a leather thong. He tested the Navy Colt then. It was several months since he had worn it, but the butt fitted his hand as smoothly as ever. The action was hair trigger and he had kept it oiled.

He dropped the revolver loosely into the holster, tried a fast draw. The gun seemed to leap into his hand, but Rosser frowned.

The years were overtaking him. His reflexes were not as fast as when he had been Marshal of Ellsworth . . . Ogallala. How many years ago had it been?

Too many.

He left his room and went out upon the street. Standing in front of the hotel he watched the stream of traffic going by. There were wagons loaded high with railroad ties; machinery, food, supplies for the railroad; horsemen, a trapper or two from the Sweetwater country; Indians who had taken to wearing white man's clothing; hard-visaged men from a score of boom towns throughout the West; lean-jawed, lean-hipped riders from the range, stolid, red-faced men from across the seas. Irishmen to work upon the railroad. Cornishmen to work in the mines. Swedes and Norwegians, who had come to settle in the north country because it was so much like their homeland.

Rosser's eyes fell upon a big two-story building a few doors away. He walked down the street, saw that the building bore a crude specimen of the sign painter's art, reading: Montana Pleasure Palace. Underneath the big sign, in straight block letters, was the name: Riley Condor.

Rosser entered.

It was a combination saloon, dance hall and gambling casino, with room enough for a dozen games and extra tables for guests. A balcony ran around three sides of the room, with doors opening off it. Eight doors, Rosser counted. Yes, Riley Condor had outdone himself.

There were two bartenders behind the long bar. Later, when the railroad

71

reached Great Plains, there would be seven or eight men behind the bar. There was room enough for them.

One of the bartenders had worked in Riley Condor's place in Broken Lance. He was polishing a glass when his eyes fell upon Tom Rosser. The glass dropped from his hand and crashed to the floor.

"Hello, Peter," Rosser said carelessly.

"Mr. Condor isn't here," the bartender blurted out. "He — he's out of town."

Rosser nodded. "That's all right. I expect to be around awhile." He made a half turn about the big saloon. "Nice place you've got here."

The bartender was unable to make a suitable reply. He reached for another glass to polish, but his hand shook so that he could not pick one up. Rosser nodded again and started for the door. Peter's eyes held on him until he passed through, then he cried out hoarsely, "Sim!"

A cold-eyed, lean man of about thirty

sauntered forward.

"That man who was just here," the bartender said, "watch him the next time he comes in. Watch him for your life."

"The old boy?" Sim asked easily. "He's somebody?"

Peter bobbed his head. "Tom Rosser!"

Sim Akins whistled softly. "Did you say *Rosser*?"

The bartender swallowed hard. "Tom Rosser, of Broken Lance, of Ogallala."

Sim Akins, whose job was to be lookout over the gambling games, when they got busy enough to require a lookout, pursed up his lips. After a moment or two, he left the saloon.

Coming out of the Montana Pleasure Palace, Tom Rosser saw a squarish log building across the street. There were iron bars across one of the windows and a newly painted sign beside the door read: Sheriff. He crossed the street and entered the log building.

A lean man, somewhat over six feet in height, sat behind a plank desk. A dismantled rifle was before him and he was peering down the heavy octagonal barrel.

He lowered the rifle barrel and his eyes met those of Tom Rosser.

"You're the sheriff?" Rosser asked.

"That's right." The sheriff got to his feet. "My name is Parker, Wes Parker."

"Tom Rosser." Rosser extended his hand.

The sheriff reached out to take it, then stopped the hand in mid-air. "Tom Rosser?"

"Yes."

Parker whistled softly. "Maybe this sheriff's job wasn't such a good idea, after all."

"It usually pays pretty well. Especially if it's a fee office."

"Oh, it's that, all right, but" — Parker's forehead creased — "you're just passing through . . . I hope?"

Rosser shook his head. "I'm figuring on staying awhile."

A frown creased the sheriff's forehead.

"If you'd come a couple of weeks sooner you'd probably gotten my badge . . . or the marshal's, if that's what you wanted."

"I don't want either job. I came to Great Plains for the same reason most people go to a new country . . . land."

The sheriff stared at Rosser. "You . . . a farmer?"

"Rancher. I've always thought I'd try my hand raising horses."

The frown remained on Parker's face. "I never heard of a lawman quitting. Usually — "

"Usually he gets killed," Rosser said quietly.

Boots pounded the wooden sidewalk outside the door and a slight young man of about twenty-five entered the Sheriff's office. A brown paper cigarette drooped from his mouth. His Stetson was tilted back from his forehead and his eyes were slitted to a squint.

"Our marshal," Wes Parker said. "Johnny Honsinger. Johnny, this is Tom Rosser."

Honsinger regarded Rosser without emotion, his eyes scarcely widening as he sized him up. "Hell," he said, "you don't look so much."

Parker said carefully, "He's taking up a ranch."

"Sure," said Honsinger carelessly. He made a flicking gesture in the general direction of Rosser's low-slung Navy gun. "Heard you stopped wearing that."

"Not yet," Rosser said.

"Well, watch yourself around here, old man," Honsinger said nastily. "You're not wearing a badge, you know."

Rosser turned to the sheriff. "See you later," he said, and walked past Honsinger, out of the Sheriff's office.

Honsinger said to the sheriff, "Hell, he's an old man."

"Old, Johnny? Yes, he must be all of thirty-eight or forty. Think you'll be alive at his age?"

"I figure to be, Sheriff," said Honsinger insolently. "I figure to be."

7

WALKING down the street, Rosser saw the sign of a livery stable and, entering the wide doorway, found the proprietor currying a fine bay gelding.

"I need a horse for a few hours," he told the man. "Wonder if you could rent me one?"

"I could, but I'd rather sell. How about this one for a hundred and ten dollars? Throw in a good saddle for twenty more."

"I'd rather rent."

"Short of money? Then how about a job? I need a man and nobody around here wants to work."

"I've got some land out in the country," Rosser said. "That's why I want to rent a horse. So I can locate the place." He took the land deed from his inside breast pocket. "Perhaps you can direct me to Section 88 . . . "

"Easy enough. Which quarter of Section 88?"

"All of it."

The liveryman showed sudden interest. "Just get to town?"

"On the morning stage."

"You say you're short of money?"

"No, *I* didn't say it. You did."

"That's right, I did. Just happens, I've been thinking of buying a little piece of land. Make you an offer for your section."

"Without even seeing it?"

"I've seen it. The land's pretty fair. Mm — six hundred and forty acres, eh? Give you a thousand dollars for it."

"The land must be a little better than fair."

"Well, fair to middling. I need some graze for my horses. Is it a deal?"

"Hardly," said Rosser. "There might be a gold mine on it."

"Uh-uh, of that I'm sure. You bought this land sight unseen, so you didn't expect much. A thousand dollars ought to be a good price to you."

"It's better than good. That's why I think I'll take a look at it."

"Twelve hundred?"

"No."

The liveryman exhaled heavily. "It was a good try. All right, mister. Your land's two miles south and one mile west . . . and since you aren't going to sell to me, I'll tell you that it's about the best damn section in this entire area. Some of the best soil in Montana. The grass on it right now is almost a foot high and there's a little stream runs smack through the middle. And not only that, but it's close in. In five years Great Plains will be at your doorstep. Hang onto the land, Mister; it's better than a gold mine. Make you more money in the long run."

Rosser was surprised. Had Jim Fell known he was deeding such a choice section to him?

The liveryman turned away, got a saddle and plunked it on the gelding. "And since you're the owner of a square mile of the best land around, I'm going to trust you. The horse — and saddle — are yours. Pay me when you get the money."

Rosser hesitated, then suddenly nodded. "That's a deal, but I'll want you to take care of the horse until I get settled."

"Good enough."

The liveryman cinched down the saddle and slipping on a bridle, handed the reins to Rosser. He mounted, winced as his stiffened muscles were extended, then rode out of the livery stable.

He rode south out of town, along a rutted trail. After two miles he came to a couple of stakes driven into the ground. One read: Section 90. Another, some fifty feet south of the first, had the figures 89 scrawled on it. Evidently a road was intended to run westward between the two stakes. He turned off the trail and rode across the gently sloping grassland.

A mile or so ahead was a clump of

cottonwoods and beyond them a taller stand of pine. He could see a winding stream off to the right.

The land was lush and verdant, well drained and well watered. It was as good grazing country as Rosser had ever seen, and when he dismounted after a few moments and scooped up a handful of earth, he saw that it was black and moist.

The liveryman had not exaggerated. The section of land was choice. He found a stake in the ground on which was scrawled '88' and knew that he stood now on his own land.

He looked around. Down there at the edge of the cottonwoods . . . no, the stream wound upland and skirted the edge of the pines. That was the place. The logs for the house and barns would not have to be hauled so far.

He mounted the gelding and put it into an easy trot. At the edge of the pines, within a hundred feet of the stream, he stopped. The house would go here. The pines would serve as a windbreak.

He cut south by west and after some fifteen minutes of searching found the west-south stake, then sighting to the north, rode in that direction. He crossed the stream in which the water was up to the gelding's belly and continuing on a quarter of a mile found the northwest stake. From here he looked over his domain. More than half of the square mile of land was wooded. The rest was grassland that would feed a considerable number of cattle, or horses. All of it was excellent for growing crops, but at the moment Rosser was not too interested in that.

This first year he would get in some cattle, a few horses. He would build his house and barns, his corral.

With what?

The twenty-one dollars in his pocket? Of course, he could sell off part of the section . . . Yet, no sooner had the thought crossed his mind than he dismissed it.

He would not sell. This was the land he had thought about during the long, lonely years, when he had never really expected that he would live long enough to hang up his gun.

This was the place he had had in mind in those rare moments when he had thought of . . . Carol Grannan.

The sun that had seemed so warm a few minutes ago had cooled off. A chill settled upon Rosser and he buttoned his coat.

He rode back to Great Plains and dismounting in front of the livery stable, led the gelding inside. The liveryman came out of the gloom of the stalls.

"The section as good as I said it was?"

"Better."

"You sure made yourself a good buy."

Rosser nodded. "Is there a bank in town?"

"Well, yes and no. Charlie Hodder's got a place goin' up, but he's been havin' a bad run of cards lately and maybe by the time the building's finished he won't be able to start a bank."

"Where am I likely to find him?"

The liveryman chuckled. "At the Pleasure Palace, where else?"

8

A POKER game, with five players, was going on in the Pleasure Palace. Rosser stopped at the bar. "Mr. Hodder here?"

The bartender pointed to the poker game. "That's Charlie there, fellow with the fancy vest."

Rosser walked to the poker game. He was within two steps of it when he came to an abrupt halt. One of the players was . . . Guy Tavenner!

Even as he stopped, Tavenner's eyes met his. "I know you," Tavenner said. "I never forget a face."

"St. Paul," Rosser said evenly. "The hotel where you — "

"Yeah," Tavenner cut in quickly. "You're the man who couldn't mind his own business . . . "

Hodder, the man with the fancy vest, threw out a hand. "Whoa, Tavenner, hold everything! We're playing poker. You want to fight, wait until after the game." He smiled up at Rosser. "Or maybe you'd rather fight it out with aces and full houses?"

"I really came over to see you, Mr. Hodder."

"Then sit down. I'm four hundred in the hole and I don't budge from here until I get it back."

"Yeah," Tavenner said nastily to Rosser, "you talk big with your mouth, let's see how big you play cards."

Rosser pulled out a chair and seated himself at the table. He brought out his entire cash resources, a crumpled ten-dollar bill, two gold half eagles and a silver dollar.

"That's all you got?" sneered Tavenner.

"It's more than you had when you quit the game the last time we played poker . . ."

"I've got more now. I'll cut you high card for that."

Rosser took out the deed to Section 88.

He handed it to Hodder. "How much will you lend me on this?"

Hodder looked curiously at Rosser, then took the deed. His eyes widened as he glanced at it. Then he folded the document and handed it back to Rosser.

"Whatever you say."

"Five hundred? A thousand?"

Hodder shrugged and Rosser turned back to Guy Tavenner. "Put up a thousand dollars."

Tavenner said sulkily, "I haven't got a thousand."

"Then how about three hundred? Isn't that the amount you beat the St. Paul hotel out of?"

Tavenner bared his teeth.

"You working for the hotel?" He counted out money, leaving a small sheaf of bills and some silver in front of him. The rest he shoved out onto the table. "There's your three hundred. When we get through cutting, win or lose, I'm going to pin your ears back for you."

Savagely, he riffled the cards and slammed the deck down on the table. Rosser reached out and shoved the pack to Hodder. "You shuffle, Mr. Hodder."

Hodder gave the cards a quick shuffle and put them down on the table. Rosser leaned over, cut the cards and turned up his cut. A ten. Tavenner sobered briefly, drew a deep breath and made a cut. He showed the seven of spades and swore roundly.

"All right, that's out of the way!" He got to his feet and kicked back his chair. "Do you want it in here or outside?"

The would-be banker, Hodder, said quietly, "Before you start, Tavenner, take a look at that deed of land."

"I'm not interested."

"You'd better be!"

Tavenner, a puzzled look on his face, but caught by the banker's tone, reached for the land deed. He flicked it open, looked at it.

"Tom Rosser," he read, then a hoarse cry was torn from his throat. "Rosser . . . the gunfighter!"

"Still want to fight?" Hodder asked thinly.

A violent shudder ran through Tavenner. He stared at Rosser, his jaw slack, his eyes threatening to bulge from their sockets. Rosser took the deed from his slack hands, put it in his pocket and began to gather up the money on the table. As he turned away, Hodder followed him.

"Mr. Rosser, I'd like to buy you a drink."

"A beer would go fine."

Hodder signaled to one of the bartenders. "Two beers."

Sim Akins came along and stopping a few feet away, glowered at Rosser. Hodder saw the lookout's face and smiled thinly.

"Have you met Mr. Rosser, Sim?"

"I've seen him," said Akins, "and I've heard of him." To Rosser: "Town's got a marshal. Nothing here for you."

"Did I ask for anything?" Rosser asked coolly.

The beers were set down for Rosser and Hodder. The latter picked up his glass and saluted Rosser. "To a quiet town."

Rosser nodded and quaffed some of his beer. Hodder set down his glass and frowned. "I think we held our election a little too soon."

"I'm not seeking any office."

"Great Plains is less than six months old and three people have already been killed in it." Hodder shook his head. "The town's getting wilder day by day and the railroad hasn't even reached us. What it'll be like when it gets here . . . " Hodder whistled softly.

"We got us a marshal," Akins said, "a man who's pretty handy with a gun hisself."

"From the things I've heard about him," Hodder said, "he's a little *too* handy with a gun."

Akins sneered openly. "I hear tell Rosser was kinda fast with a gun, his last job in Kansas . . . "

Rosser set his half-finished glass of beer on the bar and said, "I've got some things to take care of . . . " He nodded to Hodder and turning, left the saloon.

Hodder looked after him worriedly. Sim Akins moved closer to Hodder. "I also heard it said that Rosser lost his nerve, after what he did in Kansas."

Hodder turned on Akins. "What *did* he do in Kansas?"

"Killed his woman."

Hodder stared at Akins.

Rosser entered the Mountain Hotel and headed for the stairs. There was a woman at the desk, talking to the manager. Rosser's eyes flicked to her as he passed. He went three steps beyond, then stopped. He turned just as Susan Tavenner came away from the desk.

"Mrs. Tavenner!" Rosser exclaimed.

She recognized him, but she said, "I don't believe . . . "

"St. Paul."

Her eyes clouded. Her mouth opened to say something, then she changed her mind, nodded coolly and walked toward the door.

Rosser, stung, went to the stairs and ascended to the second floor. He let himself into his Room Number 4, and sat down on the bed.

In St. Paul, he had twice seen her in what must have been the most embarrassing and humiliating moments of her life. He had seen her husband strike her and he had been present when the hotel manager had evicted her, after her husband had deserted her.

"Or *had* she been deserted?

In St. Paul, she had *seemed* distraught, the deserted wife.

Yet she had lost no time in rejoining her husband.

Rosser got to his feet. What the devil was the matter with him? Why should he spend time thinking of her because she bore a slight facial and physical resemblance to a woman he had once . . . ?

He left the room.

9

DOWNSTAIRS, he crossed the hotel lobby and went out upon the veranda. The sun was sinking toward the horizon in the west and it would soon be dark, the time of the day when the enemies of Rosser prepared their plans and plots.

The railroad depot, with its huge piles of material scattered about, caught his eye and he strolled toward it.

A right of way, he noted, had already been graded up to and beyond the depot, but no ties or rails had yet been laid. There was plenty of room for sidings and beyond the depot, to the west, was a vast open area where stakes, hammered into the ground, were intended to indicate where loading pens, sidings and possibly a roundhouse would be built in the future.

A heavy-set man in shirt sleeves came out of the depot.

"Looking for a job?" he asked Rosser.

Rosser shook his head.

The man grunted. "Nobody wants to work. Everybody wants to get rich quick, buy and sell land, gamble. Nobody wants to earn it the hard way." He sized up Rosser. "Cattleman?"

"No," said Rosser, "but I've got a piece of land out of town a little way. Figure on raising some horses."

"Wish there was a horse ranch around here now. Like to buy about twenty, twenty-five good teams. Been talk about starting to lay track from here." He shook his head. "Man like Jim Fell, you never know what he's going to do. Like to have the horses ready, he makes up his mind to start eastward."

"You're in charge of operations here?" Rosser asked.

The man shrugged. "Who knows? Fell, I guess, but nobody else. I've been in charge up to now, but with Fell coming out . . . "

"He's coming to Great Plains?"

"Just got a wire from him. Left St. Paul this morning . . . " The man looked at Rosser suddenly. "You know Mr. Fell?"

"I've met him. My name's Rosser."

"How are you, Rosser? I'm Daves, Bill Daves."

They shook hands. "Don't believe I've seen you around before," Daves said.

"Just got into town today."

"What do you think of it?"

Rosser shook his head. "Too many saloons for a town this young."

Daves exclaimed, "Mister, I worked for the Union Pacific. I saw Ogallala, Julesburg, Cheyenne and Benton. I saw them when they were killing a man every hour on the hour. All those places rolled together didn't have the potential of Great Plains. There were a lot of boom towns, back in the 'sixties and 'seventies . . . cattle

96

towns, trail towns, railheads . . . Now there's only this one — the hell-spot right here, and it seems to me every gambler, every gunfighter, every short-card man and thief in the West has come here to make the last killing. Why, I've seen faces here I haven't seen in ten–fifteen years. They're older, but they're wickeder faces. Mister, Great Plains is going to be Hell, with a capital H!" Daves bobbed his head abruptly, added, "I talk too much," and walked off.

Rosser walked back up the street. He stopped before the hotel and debated as to whether to have his supper in the hotel dining room or to cross the street and eat in a little lunchroom, called Montana Eats. He decided upon the latter and crossed the street.

The place had a lunch counter, with eight stools and enough room for three tables. It was about half filled with customers. A Chinese cook could be seen through the opening that led into the kitchen. A handsome woman of about thirty was behind the counter.

She came up as Rosser took a stool. "Steak, beef stew, steak and beef stew," she said. "Coffee, tea or coffee."

"Which do you recommend?"

"Neither," the woman retorted, "the beef's tough and is all of two days old, but it's the best there is, and you look like you've got a healthy set of teeth. Better have black coffee, the milk's turning a little sour."

"You're honest," Rosser said, "so I'll leave it to you."

"Then it's the beef stew." She went to the opening into the kitchen and gave the order. She turned, looked back along the counter and came up.

"Don't I know you?"

"Ogallala," Rosser said.

"Ogallala, that's when I came out with Nellie . . ." She winced. "You were the town marshal. Rosser, Tom Rosser." A cloud came over her features. "Nine years ago, no, let's face it, eleven years ago. I — I was seventeen years old."

"You were a very pretty girl," Rosser said, then added quickly, "You've improved."

"Improved?" Bitterness came into her voice. "I've spent eleven years going from town to town, honky-tonk to — "

"You own this place?" Rosser interrupted.

"It isn't much, but what there is, I own. Every stick, every plate and saucer." She cocked her head to one side. "My name is Mary Donley. That's my real name. The one I used in Ogallala was — "

"I know."

A man who was easily six feet four, weighing in the neighborhood of two hundred and forty, got up from one of the tables and came forward. His face looked as if it had once encountered the kick of a horse, a giant Percheron.

He said, "I heard your name, Rosser."

Rosser half turned, looked over his shoulder. "Yes?"

"I wasn't in the Palace when you come in this afternoon," the big man said, "but they told me you was throwing your weight around."

"You heard wrong."

"I hope so, on account of I work for Mr. Condor and my job's throwing out people who get rough in his place." He showed blackened teeth in a sneer. My name's Flon. Remember it."

"Your bill's a dollar, Flon," snapped Mary Donley.

"I never paid more'n seventy-five cents."

"From here on it's a dollar. From you . . . "

Flon took a silver dollar from his pocket, tossed it to the counter in front of Rosser. "I got another dollar — " He started to reach into his pocket for it, but Rosser swiveled the stool around, drew his revolver and placed the muzzle against the big man's midsection.

"Don't say it!"

Flon kept his hand in his pocket and

100

looked down at the gun. "They said you was a gunslick, but me, I ain't so fast with a gun. You want to come outside?"

"No."

"Later," said Flon, "I'll catch you later. Be a pleasure." His hand still in his pocket, he turned and walked for the door.

Mary Donley called to him, as he opened the door, "Eat elsewhere hereafter!"

The door closed on Flon. Mary Donley kept her face averted a moment, then suddenly turned it to Rosser defiantly. "I'm sorry!"

"Nothing to be sorry about. Every town has its Flon."

"He broke a man's arm last week."

Rosser nodded. "He's broken some heads, too, I imagine, but someday a man half his size will send a bullet into him and Flon will be through . . . "

"Bef stoo," yelled the Chinese cook.

Mary Donley went off and brought Rosser his food. Rosser was still eating some ten minutes later when Wes Parker, the sheriff, came in and seated himself on the stool beside Rosser.

"Town's buzzing," he observed quietly.

"The big fellow who was in here a little while ago?"

"Flon? No, I hadn't heard about that." The sheriff frowned. "He's a sort of bodyguard for Riley Condor. Don't know where Condor picked him up, but he's mean . . . and strong as a buffalo bull." He paused. "Your showdown with the tinhorn, Tavenner."

"I had a brush with him in St. Paul."

"He doesn't amount to much, but Sim Akins, Condor's lookout, has been making big talk."

Rosser drank the last of his coffee. "About what?"

"Claims he backed you down." Then Parker added quickly, "he talks a lot, but he hasn't done much so far."

"I didn't like the trend of his talk,"

Rosser said slowly. "I'm new here and I didn't want to get into a fight my first day."

"That's about the way I figured it."

Rosser hesitated. "This Akins . . . he says I've lost my nerve? Is that it?"

"He was just talking."

"But that's the gist of it?"

Parker spread out his hands expressively. "I think myself he talks too much for a fighting man." He grimaced. "So does Honsinger, for that matter. But Honsinger's got a record."

"Parker," said Rosser wearily, "I've been in a lot of towns, for a good many years. I've seen all of the fancy gun boys. I met John Wesley Hardin, 'way back in 'seventy-one. I watched Wild Bill Hickok dot i's in a sign a hundred feet away. I even knew Jacob Bartles, who could shoot rings around Wild Bill. Johnny Honsinger's no better than any of those chaps."

"Probably not as good. But Wild Bill's dead — "

"Killed by a man nobody ever heard of."

"And John Wesley Hardin's in Huntsville Prison. Downed by a Texas Ranger nobody ever heard of. Pat Garrett got Billy the Kid and Wyatt Earp hung up his guns." A furrow creased Parker's forehead. "The point is, Johnny Honsinger's the best — or the worst — who's still around. At least he thinks he is, and that's important. Honsinger'd like nothing better than to go up against a — "

" — a man like me?"

Parker nodded. "He'll provoke it."

"While he's wearing a badge?"

"The badge only makes it legal." Parker hesitated again. "Condor's no friend of yours, and Honsinger's Condor's man. You know that."

"What you're trying to tell me, Parker, is that I ought to leave Montana?"

"Great Plains, at least."

Rosser took a dollar from his pocket and laid it on the counter. Mary

Donley, who had been standing a few feet away, watching Rosser and Parker, moved up.

"That's seventy-five cents, Mr. Rosser," she said.

Rosser did not hear her. He said to Parker, "I'm going to stay."

Parker let out a soft sigh. "I was afraid you were." He nodded and got to his feet.

Rosser also rose and went out of the lunchroom with the sheriff. Outside, Parker said, "Watch yourself in the tight spots."

10

PARKER went off and Rosser crossed to the hotel. He sat down in the lobby for a few minutes to let his mind run over the few things he had already learned about Great Plains.

What Jim Fell had predicted, what Rosser himself had suspected, was only too true. Condor and the men of his stripe had moved into Great Plains early. They had moved in solidly and had arrayed their strength formidably. They had elected men to public office, picking the key positions which were most liable to affect them. For all practical purposes, they ruled Great Plains.

A heavy-set man of about forty came out of a room behind the hotel desk, looked at Rosser and finally came over.

"I'm Josh Moody," he said. "I own this hotel." He held out his hand. "I'm also Mayor of Great Plains."

Rosser got to his feet and shook hands. "Rosser."

"I know. Charlie Hodder was in a little while ago. You're quite a celebrity." Moody grinned. "Question is, can the town stand another celebrity?"

"That's up to the town."

"I hope so, Rosser, I hope so." Moody exhaled heavily. "I bought into a place in Dodge, back in 'seventy-six. It was hell on hoofs. I figure this to be my last move, and I'd kinda hoped that I'd be able to get up in the morning and figure on a reasonable chance of being alive at sundown."

"I think a man has a right to expect that."

"But what do *you* think?"

"I wouldn't know, Mr. Moody — "

"Josh!"

"Josh. I just got here today."

"That's what's gnawing at me. Rosser. If I'd known your whereabouts

I'd have sounded you out two months ago about coming to Great Plains. Like I said, I've lived in Dodge City. It took Wyatt Earp, Bat Masterson, Charlie Bassett and Billy Tilghman to tame the town. We got Johnny Honsinger."

"You've also got Riley Condor."

A frown creased Moody's forehead. "Riley elected me Mayor."

"It's a nice office to hold."

"I wonder."

Susan Tavenner came out of the hotel dining room. She nodded to Moody, then added the briefest of nods to Rosser and continued on to the stairs. Moody's eyes followed her out of sight. He shook his head.

"A handsome woman! Married to a tinhorn . . . "

"I've met Mrs. Tavenner," Rosser said. "Also her husband."

"That's right. Charlie Hodder told me. Which reminds me, Charlie and some of the boys are dropping in for a little game. Care to join us?"

"I thought I'd look over the town this evening."

"We don't have a house man in our game."

"That's an inducement. I might sit in a few rounds, at that."

"Good: Boys'll be gathering in a little while. In fact, here's Joe Leach now."

Leach was the liveryman. Charlie Hodder came in on his heels and the little group moved to Moody's room behind the hotel desk, where the hotel man had set up a table and some chairs. He set out two bottles of whiskey and some glasses and by that time a lean man with drooping mustaches had joined them. He was introduced to Rosser as Norris Kent.

"Our leading sawbones," Charlie Hodder said. "In fact, he's the only one."

"I'd like to have your trade, Mr. Rosser," he said sardonically as he shook hands. "I've heard of you."

Hodder said, "You been out in the country, Doc. Tom Rosser wasn't elected marshal. He wasn't here."

"Then forgive the bad joke," the doctor apologized.

"It's all right."

The four men seated themselves at the table and played a round of draw poker. It seemed to be understood among them that the game was for table stakes and the usual bet was a dollar and two dollars, somewhat stiff, Rosser thought. Games usually began on a modest note and increased in tempo as things went along.

A fifth man joined the game after the round. He was introduced as Wendell Lewis, whose name Rosser had seen on the general store a few doors up the street.

"Stopped in at Daves' office," Lewis said, "he's expecting the big boss out day after tomorrow and figured he ought to get his books in order."

"So we're going to be honored by Mr. James Fenimore Fell," exclaimed Charlie Hodder. "Well, well!"

"Your partner," Dr. Kent said slyly.

"I wish he was!"

"Come, Charlie, you're not trying to tell me that you've got enough money to start a bank. You haven't won *that* much playing poker."

"No, but I saved my money and then last winter, my poor old aunt died and left me fifty thousand." The banker grinned. "Besides, who said anything about me putting my own money in the bank? Be taking an awful chance!"

"*I* trust you," Moody said. "You're bound to make money the way you operate. You forgot to ante up last hand and you're short again right now."

"Just for that, Josh," Hodder declared, "I open for three dollars instead of the usual dollar."

"Which means you've probably got aces or better."

The pot became a substantial one and, as it turned out, Rosser won it. He also won the next two, both of them briskly contested hands. He lost two, won a small one, lost another, then won three substantial pots in a row.

"Looks like I'm going to have a partner in the bank," Hodder observed.

"Marshal," Leach, the liveryman, said to Rosser, "these are rich men around you. But I'm only a poor liveryman. I've got horses, but very little cash. You're going to need a horse for riding, and since I find myself short of the ready, I'd like to sell you one."

"I thought I was buying the one I rode today."

"Wouldn't sell you that nag. He's for renting. Got one in the barn eating his head off. Sixteen and half hands high, built like a race horse — and runs like one."

"The chestnut, Joe?" the doctor asked.

"The same."

Kent turned to Rosser. "If there's a better horse in the territory, I haven't seen him. I'd buy him myself but he's a little too spirited for me."

"He's yours, Mr. Rosser," Leach said.

"For how much?"

Leach hesitated. "A hundred and fifty."

"That's only forty dollars more than the one I rode this afternoon. If the chestnut's that much better . . . "

"Who can pay for a good horse around here? The saloonkeepers never ride and a jackass is too fast for these city slickers . . . " he smiled warmly around the group at the table. "Present company included."

"I'll look at him in the morning."

Susan Tavenner had bolted the door and was slipping off her dress when the doorknob was suddenly turned. Startled she looked toward the door.

"Who is it?"

"Who are you expecting?" the sneering voice of Guy Tavenner asked from outside.

"Just a minute . . . "

Susan started to put the dress on again, but Tavenner rattled the doorknob impatiently. "Open up!"

Susan hesitated, then holding the

dress before her, crossed the door and shot back the bolt. Tavenner pushed in, grunted as he saw her holding the dress before her.

"I'm your husband," he said and tore the dress from her hands. He tossed it to the bed and regarded her. "You've a good figure," he conceded.

Blushing furiously, Susan retreated to the bed and sat down. Tavenner's eyes continued to look at her and it seemed to Susan that they penetrated her chemise and reached the raw flesh beneath her undergarments.

"That man in St. Paul," Tavenner said, "the Sir Galahad . . . "

"Who?"

"How many men made passes at you? Tom Rosser, who else?"

Susan made no comment, but her silence indicated plainly enough to Tavenner that she knew of whom he was speaking. And he did not like it too well.

"He's here. You've probably seen him around."

She nodded.

"Talk to him," Tavenner went on. "Find out his intentions."

"Intentions?" exclaimed Susan.

Tavenner grinned wickedly. "I want to know how long he intends to stay . . . *why* he came here . . . "

"Guy," Susan began indignantly, "I haven't exchanged two words with him."

"I didn't say you had. But I want to find out about him. Back in St. Paul he wasn't important. He may not be important now. But he *might* be." He paused. "His name's Rosser and he happens to be the best gunfighter in the West." He grimaced as he saw her react, startled. "He also happens to be Riley Condor's worst enemy. Riley's concerned about him." He stepped to the door. "Talk to him. Find out what you can from him."

"What do you want from me?" Susan cried passionately. "I've sunk about as low as a human being can go."

"I'm not asking you to bring him up here," Tavenner snapped. "I'm just asking you to play up to him. Up to a point." He jerked open the doors, started through. "Up to a point!"

11

BY ten o'clock, Tom Rosser was ahead a little more than five hundred dollars. Joe Leach pushed back his chair after Rosser had won a rather sizeable pot.

"I've lost as much as I made this week," he announced. "I'm not going to throw good money after bad."

Moody, the hotel man, yawned. I'd better relieve the night clerk awhile so he can get some grub."

The doctor, a small winner in the game, stowed away his money. "If you still want to see the town, I'll have a nightcap with you. Maybe two or three. I don't like to go to bed sober."

Rosser hesitated. He did not want to walk the streets at night in a strange town. But he nodded and left the hotel with the doctor.

Kent steered him to a saloon only a

little less large and slightly more ornate than Riley Condor's Pleasure Palace.

"Ken Rud's," he told Rosser as they entered the place. "The floors are clean now, but they won't be long. Rud likes them stained — with blood."

"Isn't he one of the city councilmen?"

Dr. Kent grunted. "I pay no attention to politics. He probably is a councilman. I expect to get a lot of business from here." He signaled to a scowling, dark-visaged man in a Prince Albert. The man came over.

"Marshal Rosser," Kent said. "Man who owns this place, Tom — Ken Rud."

"*Marshal Rosser?*" the saloonkeeper said thinly. "I was under the impression that Johnny Honsinger was elected marshal."

"Who's Johnny Honsinger?" the doctor asked cynically. "Never heard of him. Rosser's killed more men than Honsinger will ever get in front of his gun."

"Doctor," Rud said, smiling icily,

"you've a sharp tongue."

"And it's forked," the doctor chuckled. "Two fangs, like the rattlesnake." He tapped his chest and said to Rosser, "I'm a doctor, but I can't cure myself — t.b."

He caught up the bottle that the bartender brought and poured himself a glass of whiskey, which he downed in a single gulp. "This snake oil helps a little. Your health, Marshal."

"I'm not a marshal," Rosser said mildly, watching the scowling face of Rud.

"I hope you remember that," Rud growled. "Some talk that you've been leaning your weight around. I don't think the town'd like that — not when we've got an *elected* marshal and sheriff."

"This town lets me alone, I'll let it alone," Rosser said testily.

The doctor filled another glassful of whiskey, drank it with relish, then saluted Rosser with the empty glass. "I think I'm drunk enough to sleep now."

Rosser left Rud's saloon with the doctor, but outside it developed that they went in opposite directions. Rosser walked back to the hotel. As he neared the steps leading up to the veranda he saw someone standing in the shadows near the door.

His right hand dropped to his side. Then a voice spoke, "Mr. Rosser!"

Rosser climbed the stairs, took a step to the right, out of the direct light from inside the hotel lobby. "Mrs. Tavenner . . ."

"I've been rude to you," Susan Tavenner said. "In St. Paul as well as here. You've tried to be kind and I've responded horribly."

"It's all right, Mrs. Tavenner," said Rosser.

"It isn't all right," she exclaimed poignantly. "Things haven't been well for some time. Guy's had a bad run of luck."

"All gamblers have them."

"It's true? There are good times and bad . . . ?"

"Of course."

"Guy says that Great Plains will be a prosperous place. He — he believes his luck will turn. I've heard about you, Mr. Rosser. You're an officer of the law . . . "

"Not any more."

"Then why did you come to Great Plains?"

Rosser hesitated. "I have a farm outside of town, a ranch, I guess you would call it. I plan to settle on it."

"Then you didn't come here to — to fight people like — like my husband or Mr. Condor?"

Rosser could not restrain a weary exhalation. "Mrs. Tavenner, did your husband ask you to question me?"

A low cry was torn from her. "You — you think *that*?"

"What am I to believe? I had a — a disagreement with your husband this afternoon. He then learned my identity — "

"What *is* that identity?" she demanded fiercely.

"You name it, Mrs. Tavenner . . . "

"All right, I will. You're a killer. They — they say the worst in the history of the West. You hide behind a lawman's badge and wreak your personal vengeance against the people you dislike and that means anyone who dares to oppose you and your desires."

"You say that, Mrs. Tavenner, because your husband told you so and you love your husband . . . "

"It's the truth, isn't it?"

"I'll tell you the truth, Mrs. Tavenner — "

"Stop calling me Mrs. Tavenner. You — you make it sound like a dirty word."

"The truth," Rosser said, "is that I hate men of the stripe of Riley Condor . . . "

"And Guy!"

"Guy," Rosser said, no longer trying to conceal his contempt. "Guy Tavenner's a cheap tinhorn gambler. A man who uses his wife to — "

Her hand came up in the semidarkness and gave his cheek a resounding slap. Rosser uttered a low cry and took a backward step.

"How dare you!" she blazed. "How dare you talk to me like that!" Her hand came up to strike him again, but he reached out and caught it. He found it a surprisingly strong hand — and warm.

"I think," he said bleakly, "we have nothing more to say to each other." He released her hand and, turning, walked into the hotel.

He clumped up the stairs to his room and threw himself on the bed without undressing. He lay for long hours, staring sightlessly at the ceiling. A heaviness settled over him that was still upon him when daylight finally lighted up his room.

He took off his shirt, washed himself and donned a fresh shirt. He descended to the lobby and found that it was too early for breakfast.

He stepped out upon the veranda

and looked down the street. A man was sweeping the wooden sidewalk in front of a store and a half-dozen horses were tied to the hitchrails, but otherwise the street was deserted. His eye caught sight of the livery stable diagonally across the street and on a sudden impulse he crossed to it.

A rheumy-eyed oldster sat dozing in a cubbyhole just inside the door. He blinked owlishly as Rosser stopped in the door.

"Yes, sir. What stall?"

"I haven't got a horse here, but I stopped in to look at one that Joe Leach said he'd sell me."

"Not Alexander!"

"A bay sixteen and a half hands high. Joe said it was the fastest horse in the territory — "

"That's Alexander, all right . . . "

The night hostler got to his feet and led Rosser to a box stall. "Here he is. Leach doesn't think any more of this horse than he does of his right arm. Man plunked down four hundred dollars for him last week and Leach wouldn't even listen . . . "

"Four hundred? He offered him to me for a hundred and fifty."

"Uh-uh, you didn't hear right. Couldn't been Alexander he was talking about . . . "

Rosser entered the stall. The horse snorted and stamped about, but Rosser had a way with horses and quieted him easily. He ran his hands down the magnificent animal's flanks and even picked up a hoof. The horse was built for speed, a trifle taller than the ordinary race horse, but with an exceedingly deep chest that indicated stamina. He had powerful hocks.

Long before he completed his examination of Alexander, Rosser knew that he had to own this horse. Money was no object. He would give every dollar he had in his pocket and more.

He came out of the stall to meet Joe Leach descending a ladder from a room over the stable. He was in his undershirt, but he had put on his trousers and boots.

"Heard you," he said. "Like him?"

"He's all you said he was."

"He's more, Rosser."

"How much?"

"What I said last night. A hundred and fifty."

Rosser's eyes went to the night hostler. "Didn't someone offer you four hundred for him?"

"Some people talk too much." Leach scowled at the hostler. "Get back to your nap, Amos."

The hostler went off and Leach dropped his voice to a confidential whisper. "Horse has a little flaw . . . "

Rosser looked back into the stall. Leach chuckled. "Won't see it. He can't stand to have any other horse pass him."

"That's a flaw?"

"Could be sometimes."

Rosser frowned. "Why do you want to sell him to me for a hundred and fifty dollars?"

"Because you need a horse."

Rosser shook his head. "I don't need charity."

"All right, pay me more."

"Three hundred?"

"He's yours."

Rosser continued to frown. "For some reason you're trying to place me under an obligation."

"No obligation, I need the money. You need the horse. That's all there's to it."

Leach's words could not be weighed. But his character could be.

Rosser said, "You know that I have some property here — "

"I made you an offer for it."

"You also know that I did not come to Great Plains to take the marshal's job."

"Couldn't have it, anyway. Marshal here's elected and Johnny Honsinger's already got the job."

"Then, why? What do you want from me?"

"Your friendship."

"That's all?"

127

"That hard to believe, Rosser?"

"I won five hundred dollars last night . . ."

"About what I lost."

"I won it from you, Josh Moody, Doctor Kent and Wendell Lewis."

"We'll get it back, don't worry."

Rosser made a sudden decision. "I'll buy the horse from you. For the five hundred dollars I won last night."

"You own Alexander."

"I also want a saddle."

"Alexander's private saddle goes with him."

Rosser paid out the money and Joe Leach wrote out a bill of sale. Rosser could not relieve himself of the feeling that he had somehow been trapped into something, but he wanted Alexander and he had paid an honest price for him.

He saddled the horse and with Joe Leach watching, mounted him and rode out upon the street. He trotted the magnificent horse out to open country, then gradually put him into a fast run, winding up in a gallop.

Rosser had never ridden as fast as this in his life and when he finally turned the horse and sent him back toward Great Plains, the animal was breathing only a little more heavily than normal.

He took the horse back to the stable. Leach was gone, but he turned him over to Amos, the hostler. "He's all you said he was and more."

"He sure is, Mr. Rosser."

"Rub him down and feed him."

When he stepped out of the stable, Rosser saw the sheriff, Wes Parker, bearing down on him.

"Saw you riding Alexander," the sheriff remarked. "Surprised Leach would let you ride him."

"I bought him."

Parker looked at him sharply. "Everybody in Great Plains has tried to buy that horse from Leach. He wouldn't sell."

"He lost some money in a game last night."

"Much?"

"What I paid for the horse."

"How much was that?"

Rosser grinned. "You one of the people who tried to buy Alexander?"

"Why not?"

"All right, Sheriff, I paid five hundred dollars. What I won last night and what Leach lost."

"I offered him as much. Leach must have taken a liking to you. Or else . . . "

"Or?"

"Leach plays cards with Charlie Hodder and Josh Moody."

"I suppose that means something."

Parker grimaced. "They're what you might call the respectable element in this town . . . "

"Charlie Hodder played poker yesterday at Riley Condor's."

"Yes, but he also plays with Josh Moody and Joe Leach — privately." Parker nodded thoughtfully. "Had you been here before the elections, they would have tried to persuade you to run for marshal . . . or sheriff."

"But the elections are over."

"They still want you on their side, that's apparent."

"Sheriff," said Rosser, "you keep talking about sides . . . are there *sides* in this town?"

"Now *you're* being cagey, Rosser."

"Which side are you on, Sheriff?"

"That's a good question. I've even asked it of myself. I came to town two months ago and someone suggested I put my name up for sheriff . . . "

"Who suggested it?"

"Not Riley Condor. He wasn't here at the time." Parker nodded toward Rud's saloon. "Ken Rud. And to save you time, I'll answer the next question. Yes, Rud and Condor are as thick as — as thieves. I can only add to that, that I knew Rud slightly some years ago down in — in Dodge City."

"You were in Dodge?"

"Passing through. I was driving a herd from Denton, Texas, to Wyoming. Rud had a place in Dodge City." Parker smiled crookedly. "Next question?"

Rosser shook his head. "I've asked about three more questions than I have a right to ask of a man I've only known for a day."

"All right," Parker said cheerfully. "Now answer just *one* question for me? Why are you in Great Plains?"

Rosser shook his head. "You don't like the answer I gave you yesterday?"

"Not especially."

"Does it make any difference to you?"

"Not to me. It might to some other people."

"I wonder what kind of breakfast Mary Donley serves," Rosser said evenly.

"Very good. I'll join you."

12

MARY DONLEY greeted them warmly and Rosser soon found that Parker had not overstated Mary's qualifications. He ate a stack of pancakes and followed with an order of ham and eggs that satisfied him more than anything he had eaten in months.

As they left the restaurant, Flon came toward them across the street. He was grinning wickedly. "Riley's back," he said, as he came up.

"That's supposed to mean something?" Rosser asked.

"He wants to talk to you."

"I'm staying at the hotel."

"Uh-uh," said Flon, "he wants you should come to his place."

"I just told you, I'm staying at the hotel."

"You're pretty big," said Flon, "but

take off the gun and I'll *take* you to Riley."

"Why don't you try taking the gun from me?" Rosser challenged.

Flon smiled at the sheriff. "You see, Sheriff, he's trying to make trouble . . ."

"Seems to me you're the one looking for the fight," Parker said sourly.

"Me? Why, I don't even carry a gun."

"You crippled a man less than two weeks ago."

"With my bare hands."

"You're not going to break any of my bones," Rosser said warmly. "I'm warning you about that right now. You touch me and I'll put a bullet into you."

"See, Sheriff?"

"Go back to Condor," the sheriff said, "tell him Mr. Rosser refuses to see him."

"No," said Rosser, "I'll go to him."

A sneer twisted Flon's lips. He turned and trotted back to the Pleasure Palace. Rosser looked inquiringly at Parker, then started after Flon.

A heavy exhalation was torn from the sheriff's throat and he followed Rosser, who slackened his pace so that Parker fell in beside him.

"You don't have to come."

"I know about you and Condor. You were enemies back in Kansas."

"Someday," Rosser said, "I'm going to kill Condor."

"Not today?"

"I'll choose the time and the place. When there's just Condor and me."

"That's fair, Rosser. I don't know what there is between you and Condor, but I've heard rumors — "

"Let it ride, Sheriff!"

They had reached the Pleasure Palace. Without hesitation, Rosser pushed open the door and went inside. He heard Parker's footsteps behind him.

It was a stakeout, of course. Sim Akins and another man were at the bar; two gun-carrying men were at the right of the room, not too far back and Flon was just outside the door of Condor's office, which stood open. Three men were carelessly watching from the balcony that went around three sides of the huge room.

Rosser barely glanced around the room, then stepped to the bar, a few feet from Sim Akins.

"Tell your boss I'm here."

"Tell him yourself."

"He sent for me. I've come this far."

"Then go the rest of the way."

"Your job," Rosser said deliberately, "may be shooting people in the back. I don't want to make it too easy for you."

"You're asking for it, Rosser!"

"Not from you, I'm not. You won't stand up and fight . . ."

"Don't be too sure of that." Akins scowled at Rosser. "I haven't heard of you facing any *man* lately."

The inference was plain enough, but Rosser had been expecting a taunt to snap him into gunplay — gunplay that would be his finish. He said, "Condor tell you to say that to me?"

"*I'm* saying it."

Condor stepped out of his office. He gave Rosser a half salute.

"Rosser!"

"You wanted to see me, Condor?"

Condor came forward, his face twisted into a frozen smile. "Heard you were in town. Always want to see my old friends."

"We're friends, Condor?"

"This is a new year, a new town — "

"And a new deal?"

Condor shrugged. "You're calling it."

"Any deck you're dealing is a crooked one, Condor."

The frozen smile on Condor's face became a little more solid. "You're laying it on the line."

"That's right, Condor. You don't dare kill me with this many witnesses, but you'll try to get me in the dark when I least expect it. I know that . . . I also know that I'm going to kill you in the end."

"You're making that threat in front of

137

these same witnesses." Condor looked past Rosser at Wes Parker. "You heard him, Sheriff."

"I heard him," said the sheriff.

Sim Akins took a forward step. "You're talkin' mighty big for an old — "

That was as far as he got. Rosser smashed him savagely in the face with his fist. Akins went back against the bar, caromed from it to the floor. He rolled over, struggled to his knees and groped for his gun.

He got the weapon clear and Parker kicked it from his hand. "There'll be no gunplay here," he announced. He drew his own revolver and sent a quick look around the room. "Call in your dogs, Mr. Condor."

The smile was finally gone from Condor's face. He made a small gesture with his right hand, his eyes still on Rosser. "You said your piece, Rosser."

"I think we understand each other."

Rosser turned and walked carelessly out of the Pleasure Palace.

13

LEAVING Condor's Pleasure Palace, Rosser walked to the hotel. He climbed to his room, entered and locked the door. He took off his coat and extended his right hand. It trembled violently.

He shook his head. He had been in no real danger. Riley Condor had made the stakeout only to impress him. He would never have Rosser shot down in broad daylight, in his own saloon.

A hotel corridor at night. A shot in the dark that was Riley Condor's trademark. A hired assassin, like the man from Idaho, back in Broken Lance.

The man from Idaho.

Rosser had spent a month in Idaho, the previous winter. A man named Lee Ring had left his old stamping grounds in the Hole-in-the-Wall country late in September and had not returned. That much he had learned. But Lee Ring was only a name. The people who knew the name could not describe Ring and those who knew him were as hard to find as Lee Ring himself. Even if Rosser had found them, they were not the kind who would talk.

Rosser removed his boots and stretched out upon the bed. He had dozed only for minutes at a time during the night. He was bone-weary, yet he could not sleep. His mind kept wandering . . .

Not to the scene at the Pleasure Palace, but to the woman who had accosted him the night before on the veranda of the hotel.

Susan Tavenner.

He had known her for less than a week, yet he could recall every line of her face, every curve of her mouth, her nostrils. She was so much like Carol Grannan.

"No," he suddenly said aloud, then wincing, rolled over on his side.

Carol Grannan was dead. She was

the only woman he had ever loved in his life, the only woman he would ever love.

And she was dead.

Ken Rud entered the Pleasure Palace, gave it a critical survey and walked along the bar to Riley Condor's office. The door was tightly closed and he knocked on it.

"Come," called a voice from inside.

Rud entered and found Condor seated in his swivel chair, turned away from his desk. Harold Price, who owned the Nugget Saloon and Fred Wagoner of The High Country were seated on straight-backed chairs.

"Come in, Ken," Condor greeted Rud. "Meeting's just getting started."

"Council?" Rud asked with heavy sarcasm.

"Don't see the mayor, do you?" Price said.

"Tom Rosser's in town," Condor said, by way of opening proceedings.

"He was in my place last night," Rud

141

said. "Came in with Doctor Kent."

"He didn't lose any time getting in with that crowd," observed Condor. "It's my hunch that they sent for him."

"What good will that do?" demanded Rud. "Rosser has no official status. We held an election. We've got a marshal, a judge and a sheriff. Rosser steps out of line we throw the book at him." Rud's lip curled. "The good-citizen crowd can't do a damn thing."

"That's the point of this meeting," declared Condor. "Moody and his crowd may have sent for Rosser, but I think we — the town council and the elected officials — can get rid of him."

"How?" asked Price, the owner of the Nugget Saloon.

Condor looked thoughtfully around the ring of faces. Then he reached under his Prince Albert and produced a revolver.

"That's the best way," said Rud.

Price looked worriedly at Condor.

"I'm against killing . . . except as a last resort."

Condor pursed up his lips, then shifted to Wagoner, who had not yet spoken. "Fred?"

"I side with Harold," Wagoner said. "I don't favor killing . . . "

"Now, wait a minute," Rud snapped. "We had this out before. We made up a pool and we rigged an election. We decided it was our last big chance for a cleanup. We've got to make our pile in Great Plains."

"We're going to, Ken," said Condor.

"I'll go along," said Wagoner, "up to cold-blooded murder."

"That's good enough," Condor said tightly. "I know Rosser better than any of you. The man's a killer. He killed his own sweetheart down in Kansas and if we just stand still, he'll overstep himself again. Then we'll crack down on him. We're the law in this town."

"Let it rest there!"

Wagoner got up from his chair. He started for the door, his forehead creased in worry. At the door he stopped, then shook his head and went out. Price, his lips pursed into a tight pout, followed.

Rud waited until the two others had left, then said to Condor, "You and me, Riley, are going to have to handle things."

Condor shook his head. "It's not good, Ken. The town's growing pretty fast. People coming in every day, businesses starting up all the time. We need strength."

"There're others besides Price and Wagoner."

"They were here before we were. We need them to bring the newcomers into line."

"We've got to get rid of Rosser. They'll fall into line if there's no one to fight their battles for them."

About the time Ken Rud left the Pleasure Palace, Josh Moody climbed the stairs to the second floor of his hotel and knocked on the door of Room Number 4.

"Tom?" he called. "Josh Moody."

There was only silence in the room. Moody knocked again and heard the creaking of bedsprings. He twisted the doorknob. That brought results.

Rosser's voice, inside, said, "Just a minute."

The door was opened by Rosser.

"Hello, Josh."

Moody came in and closed the door. "Heard about the ruckus at Condor's."

"Nothing came of it," Rosser said carelessly. "Condor was just trying to show me his strength. Some of it."

"Perhaps," said Moody. He picked up the straight-backed chair, turned it around and seated himself, resting his chin on the chair back. "Condor's the leader, isn't he?"

"He was in Broken Lance, Kansas, and I imagine he is here."

Moody nodded thoughtfully. "It was Condor who kept talking about the election. He fixed it. Made me mayor to get me to go along, then elected his pals to the council. Nominally,

145

I'm head of the town government, but they can outvote me on anything any time."

"What's the judge like?"

"Pete Murcott?" Moody wrinkled his nose in disgust. "All the law he knows he picked up when he served on a jury once back East. He spends most of his time in the saloons. And that marshal, Honsinger — "

"I know about him." Rosser hesitated. "What about the sheriff?"

"He's quiet, minds his own business, but I've heard talk that Ken Rud brought him here. Aside from that, I'd say he was a pretty good man." Moody paused. "The boys and I have talked things over. We'd like you on our side."

"What side is that?"

Moody made a small gesture of annoyance. "The side that's opposed to the saloonkeepers. The decent element — if we aren't bragging by calling ourselves that. The businessmen. You met some of them last night."

"Josh," Rosser said carefully, "I'm not going to align myself with any side or faction."

"But Condor's your mortal enemy!" cried Moody.

Rosser nodded. "And I'm going to kill him one day, if he doesn't kill me first." He shook his head. "I hate Condor and all his kind. I'll fight them whenever and wherever I can — but I'm not going to tie myself down to the Good Government, the Decent Citizens or any other group."

"That wasn't what we had in mind," Moody said stiffly. "Montana has a precedent . . . Virginia City . . . "

"Vigilantes?" Rosser stared at Moody.

"They were necessary in 'sixty-four. The way things are shaping up in Great Plains, Virginia City and Alder Gulch will seem like tea parties."

"I don't approve of vigilantes," Rosser said slowly.

"Nobody approves of them," snapped Moody. "Colonel Sanders, who headed the vigilantes in 'sixty-four, didn't approve of them. But they were necessary. The law was in with the road agents. Nobody wants vigilantes here, but can we sit by and watch a gang of thieves and cutthroats take over our town?"

"Hold off your vigilantes," Rosser said soberly. "Hold off until — "

He stopped. Boots pounded the floor outside, then the door was kicked in violently. Johnny Honsinger, gun in hand, stormed into the room.

"Old man," he cried, "I warned you not to throw your weight around in this town!"

"What are you talking about?" demanded Rosser.

"Condor's — you were down at Condor's a while ago — "

"Marshal," interrupted Moody, "wait a minute. I heard what happened at Condor's — "

"So did I. This old boy came in and started knockin' people around. That don't go in my town."

"*Your* town?" demanded Moody.

"I was elected marshal," Honsinger said thinly. "I got no boss. Not even you, Mr. Mayor."

"I think it's time someone corrected you," Moody said warmly. "We've all of us got bosses. The people."

"The people elected me!"

"They can also throw you out of office. You're responsible to them. Besides — your duties are to *enforce* the laws, not make them. You can arrest a lawbreaker, but you have to bring him before a court of law."

"All right, then I'm arresting Rosser."

"Don't be a fool, Honsinger," snapped Moody. "Even Condor wouldn't prefer charges against Rosser for what happened in his place. Ask him."

Honsinger hesitated, glowering. "I warned you, old man," he finally said to Rosser. "I don't want you in this town in the first place, but as long as you're here, you'll toe the mark. I ain't afraid of you and your rep don't impress me a damn, understand?"

"I understand," Rosser said wearily.

Honsinger glowered again, gave Moody a nasty look and went out. Moody exhaled heavily. "And that's our law-enforcement arm!" He, too, went out.

14

THE giant, Flon, stood outside the Pleasure Palace and saw Rosser come out of the hotel and cross the street to Mary Donley's restaurant. He chuckled wickedly, hitched up his belt and headed for the restaurant.

Rosser was seated at the counter, talking to Mary when Flon came in.

"Well, this is a nice, cozy place," Flon said loudly.

"It was," Mary said coldly, "until you came in. I told you you could take your business elsewhere — "

"Oh, sure, I can eat anywhere," Flon said wickedly. "Only I didn't come here to eat." He took two silver dollars from his pocket. "I got two dollars here, and I'd like two dollars' worth of the best you've got." He smirked. "And I don't mean grub."

Rosser wheeled on the stool. "Flon, I warned you the last time . . . "

"Sure," Flon said wickedly, "you're gonna shoot me — even if I haven't got a gun." He reached past Rosser, scooped up a plateful of oatmeal and slammed it into Rosser's face.

He stepped back, a crooked grin on his ugly features.

No man could take what Rosser had just taken. He dashed the breakfast food from his face with one hand and with the other struck Flon in the face.

Flon took the punch easily. "Well, well," he said, "the man wants to fight."

"Don't, Tom!" cried Mary Donley. "That's what he wants."

"Too late," sang out Flon. "He hit me first."

He stepped forward. Rosser slid off the stool and backed away against a chair and table. He gripped the chair, whipped it around and crashed it down over Flon's head.

A shudder ran through the big man, but he withstood the blow that would have felled a lesser man. A groan of despair was torn from Rosser's throat. He leaped forward, smashed Flon on the jaw, a blow so hard that pain shot through Rosser's arm all the way to his shoulder. His left he sank into Flon's stomach and there he found not too much resistance. The big fellow had been living too soft of late. The ridge of muscle in his stomach was becoming flabby.

A ray of hope flickered in Rosser. He brought his right into the stomach before him. And then his head seemed to explode. Flon's fist had caught him a glancing blow. It was enough to send Rosser back, crashing over one of Mary Donley's tables. Flon lumbered forward, brushed aside the wreckage of the table and caught Rosser getting to his knees. He kicked Rosser in the stomach and as Rosser bent foward, gasping, he kicked him in the head.

Rosser went over sidewards, barely conscious. Flon's thick lips twisted in pleasure and he moved in for his specialty, kicking a man to death.

Then Mary Donley rose up from behind the lunch counter. A short, double-barreled shotgun was in her hands. As she elevated the muzzle she sent one blast into the ceiling.

Flon, his foot raised to kick Rosser, turned. "Put that down," he said thickly.

"The next blast takes off your head," Mary said coldly.

"You'll be sorry," Flon said. "I'll catch you without the gun sometime."

"I'll count three. One — "

Flon headed for the door. Instinct told him that Mary would do exactly as she said — blow off his head.

As the door slammed, Rosser stirred. A groan of pain came from his lips. Mary Donley thrust the shotgun at one of the patrons who had crowded to the rear of the lunchroom.

"Get Doctor Kent!"

A half hour later, Doctor Kent finished daubing Rosser's head wound with iodine. "Next time you feel in need of exercise," he said, "go out and tackle a Montana grizzly. He won't hurt you as much as Flon."

"Flon won't touch me again," Rosser said. "I'll shoot him the moment he makes another threatening move."

"Maybe that's what Condor wants," Kent said, sober for the moment.

Rosser looked at him. "Perhaps it is."

Leaving Great Plains at an easy canter, Rosser gradually let out Alexander and by the time they had gone a half mile the fine animal was in a full gallop. His speed was terrific and Rosser, feeling the cooling breeze on his face, knew that he had never ridden such a magnificent animal.

Suddenly, he became aware of a horse ahead of him and pulled up Alexander. As he came up with the other rider he saw that it was Susan Tavenner. She recognized him and moved her horse aside.

He nodded coolly and was about to pass her, when she spoke. "Mr. Rosser?"

He pulled Alexander to an abrupt halt, started to turn, but she rode up to him. "I'm glad you came along," she said clearly. "I — I want to apologize for the other night."

"No apology is necessary."

"I'm afraid it is," she said, "because you were quite right. I *was* trying to pump you."

"Mrs. Tavenner," Rosser said, "I'm out for a ride. Shall we just talk about that?"

A half smile, the first he had ever seen, came over her face. "Let's!"

She started her horse forward and Rosser kneed Alexander to keep alongside of her mount.

"Didn't think you went in for riding," he remarked.

"I rode back home," she retorted. "I can't sit in the hotel all day." Then: "That's a fine horse you're riding."

"You're a good judge," Rosser said,

pleased. "Best horse I ever rode."

"Does he have a name?"

"Alexander."

"Alexander?" She half smiled. "Perhaps he should be called Bucephalus. I've been hearing things about you."

He grimaced. "I'm no conqueror. I've been a peace officer, but now — " He indicated the stakes ahead. "Like to turn here with me? I'll show you something."

She followed him down the line of stakes and a few minutes later sat her horse beside him on the grassy knoll overlooking the stream.

"This is where I'm going to build my house," he said. "I hope to spend every evening of the rest of my life looking down at that stream — and seeing my barns, my corrals, my horses grazing. Over there, I'll make a special corral for the colts and yearlings. They'll be able to get into the big barn whenever the weather turns bad."

"A man's ranch," Susan said thoughtfully. "I note you didn't mention henhouses, or a spring house . . . "

"No," he said, "I didn't."

"Why not?"

"I was planning to live here by myself."

"Oh!" she said. Then, after a moment's silence, "What was her name?"

"Carol," he replied before he caught himself.

"Carol," she said, "it's a nice name. Am I prying, if I ask what happened between you and Carol?"

"No," he said harshly. "It's matter of public record. The newspaper printed it. I killed her."

A low cry was torn from Susan. "That's impossible!"

"Why? I'm a professional killer. That's been my vocation ever since I remember."

"You were a law officer!"

"Same thing. Pin a badge on a man and it makes his killings legal, that's all."

"But this — this Carol. She

couldn't have been . . . "

"According to the newspapers," Rosser said carefully, "I'd had a quarrel with Carol Grannan and killed her."

"According to the newspapers," Susan repeated, "but what was the *real* story?"

"That's no longer important," Rosser said bleakly. "What was between Carol Grannan and myself — was between us. The world says it was something else. But I know." He paused. "And I think *she* knows."

Susan turned her horse away, rode down to the edge of the stream. She looked across it and after a while, Rosser joined her.

"Ready to go back to town?"

"Yes. I — I think your ranch is going to be a wonderful place."

"Thanks."

They were almost back to Great Plains when she said, "You must have been very much in love with Carol." He made no reply and she put her horse into a gallop, all the way back to town.

Rosser rode slowly and when he turned Alexander in to the livery stable, Susan was already gone.

Joe Leach himself took care of Alexander.

"Like him?"

"I've never had a horse like him."

"As for that," said Leach, "I never owned one like him." He shrugged. "My loss, your gain."

15

RILEY CONDOR was laying out a solitaire game when Flon entered his office.

"You wanted me, boss?"

Condor played a few cards before speaking. Then he said, "You had a fight with Rosser."

"Wasn't much of a fight."

"The girl in the restaurant stopped you from kicking in his brains."

"I'll catch her without a shotgun one of these days."

"That'll be nice," said Condor. "Just about your size."

Flon finally understood. "Whaddya want me to do — kill Rosser?"

"You're not man enough!"

"I'm not afraid of any man in the world," Flon said heavily. "Only thing I can't handle is a gun. I tried that once." He held up his huge hands.

161

"My hands are too big."

"Rosser's giving me trouble," Condor said evenly. "I don't want him gunned, but I want him licked — the way you started to do this morning . . . "

"Next time I see him," said Flon eagerly. "Fact, I'll look him up right now."

"He won't fight you again."

"I'll *make* him fight!"

"No," said Condor. "It's got to look right. He'll have to attack you. Hit the first blow . . . "

"He did this morning . . . "

"After you threw the oatmeal in his face." Condor shook his head. "He's got to hit the first blow."

"He won't!" cried Flon.

"Used to be a man back home," Condor said, "regular saint. Took the collection in church on Sundays and spent most of his time reading the Bible. Didn't drink, didn't smoke, never used bad language. Man came along one day and kicked his dog. Holy Joe just about killed him. Some people

162

are that way about animals."

A gleam came into Flon's eyes.

At seven thirty in the evening Riley Condor came out of his office. He looked over the big room and saw Guy Tavenner preparing his faro layout.

"You," he called. "Tavenner!"

Tavenner looked up, frowned, then rose and came across the room. "Yes, Riley."

Condor took out his big gold watch and looked at it. "Find your friend, Tom Rosser — "

"He's no friend of mine."

"Find him anyway. At exactly seven forty-five tell him to hurry over to the livery stable and take a look at his horse."

Tavenner scowled. "You could send one of the bartenders to do that."

"I'm sending you. Start now."

It was in Tavenner's mind to tell Riley Condor to go to hell, but his courage wasn't that big. He left the Pleasure Palace, and clomped to the

163

hotel. Rosser was in the lobby, reading a week-old St. Paul newspaper.

Tavenner looked at the wall clock behind the hotel desk. It read seven thirty-eight. Tavenner stalked past Rosser and climbed the stairs to the second floor. He rattled the door of his wife's room.

She opened it and Tavenner scowled when he saw that she was fully dressed.

"Where do you think you're going?" he demanded.

"Down to dinner."

"You'd think you could eat earlier."

"The dining room's open until eight thirty."

"All right, go and eat," he snapped. He turned his back on Susan and stalked off. He heard her close the door and follow him. He did not wait for her, however.

Down in the lobby he saw that it was close enough. Seven forty-two. He went over to Rosser.

"Better get over to the barn and look at that horse of yours," Tavenner snapped.

Rosser regarded him sharply. "Why?"

"Because I'm telling you. And now!"

Rosser got to his feet, saw Susan coming down the stairs. He hesitated, then turned and went out of the hotel.

It could be a trap.

In the falling darkness he headed for the livery stable. He approached it, his hand swinging close to the butt of his revolver.

There was a light on inside the stable — a dim lantern. As he stepped into the open doorway he saw by the lantern light that a body was sprawled on the floor. The oldster who took care of the stable at night.

It was a trap.

Rosser started to back away. Then a horse in a stall whickered. A hoof stamped and a man swore angrily. It was in Alexander's stall. Rosser's hand dropped to his gun.

A horse suddenly screamed — a scream of terrible anguish. It continued to scream, although it was momentarily cut off as a huge body thudded to the stable floor.

Flon came out of the stall. Rosser recognized him even in the dim light . . . Flon, holding a dripping knife in his hand.

"Flon!" Rosser said hoarsely.

"The big gunfighter," sneered Flon, starting toward Rosser. "I just fixed your horse — hamstrung him." Deliberately, he threw away his knife. "Gonna fight me?"

For one awful moment Rosser was sick at his stomach. Then something seemed to explode within him. He was not even aware that he drew his gun, that the explosion that rocked the livery stable came from his gun.

But Flon was staggering. "You — you shot me!" he gasped. "Condor told me . . . " That was as much as he got out. He fell forward on his face, twitched once or twice, then lay still.

People appeared in the livery stable behind Rosser. He was not even aware of them. He walked stiffly to the stall in which Alexander lay. He saw what Flon had done to the magnificent animal and pointed his gun at the horse's head. He pulled the trigger twice, then came out of the stall.

Joe Leach grabbed his arm. "Migawd," he said. "You killed Flon!"

"He crippled Alexander," Rosser said dully.

Leach looked into the stall, turned back, shuddering. "Man'd do a thing like that . . . "

Johnny Honsinger came striding into the stable. His gun was in his hand. "Drop it old man," he cried. "Drop it, or try using it!"

Rosser looked at the revolver hanging loosely in his hand. His eyes went up toward Honsinger saw that the young gunfighter was tense, eager. He *wanted* to kill Rosser.

Rosser let the gun fall from his hand.

Honsinger came forward. "You gave up," he said, disappointed. Then his eyes fell on Flon's body. "You killed him!"

"I killed him," Rosser said.

"You're under arrest," cried Honsinger. "Throw up your hands."

"Stop it, Honsinger," said Leach. "You can't arrest Rosser."

"Let's see somebody try to stop me. *You* want to try it, Leach?" He half turned to Josh Moody, who was coming in. "You want to try, Mr. Mayor?"

Moody did not like what he saw in the young marshal's eyes and came toward Rosser.

"Better surrender, Tom," he said quickly. "We'll get it straightened out later."

Honsinger bared his teeth in a wicked grin. "Man gets caught murdering somebody he generally gets straightened out — at the end of a rope." He came forward, waved at Rosser with the muzzle of his revolver. "Come along, old man."

Rosser drew a deep breath and started toward the door. Honsinger scooped up Rosser's gun and fell in behind him. "To the calaboose," he ordered, "and keep those hands up all the way."

Rosser marched to the jail building. There was a single cell behind the sheriff's and marshal's office, and Honsinger herded him into this.

"This'll keep you nice and cozy until the Judge gets time for you," he said sardonically. He slammed the door and turned the key on the office side.

Rosser looked about the cell. It was about nine by twelve feet in size, with a single barred window at the rear. There were two wooden bunks in the room, with a single, new blanket on each. There had been very few — if any — previous prisoners.

Rosser sat down on one of the bunks. His mind was clearing and he ran through the sequence of events of the last few minutes.

He shook his head. Flon had crippled his horse, had advanced on him with the bloody knife in his hand . . . No, he had thrown away the knife.

He had actually been unarmed at the instant that Rosser had drawn his revolver and shot him.

Although, *was* Flon actually ever disarmed? His fists alone were lethal weapons. Rosser had gone up against them only that morning. Had he not been stopped by Mary Donley, Flon might even have killed Rosser.

The key rattled in the door. It was pulled open and Parker stood framed in the doorway, in the lamplight of the room behind him.

"What's the story, Rosser?" he asked. "I've heard six versions in the last ten minutes. Like to hear it from you."

Rosser told him as closely as he could, adding, "Condor's work. He sent Flon to hamstring my horse, then sent Tavenner to warn me — so I'd catch Flon in the act."

"You don't know that for sure?"

"In my own mind I'm sure."

Sheriff Parker frowned. "I'm wondering how it'll sound in Judge Murcott's court."

"Murcott's not much of a judge, I'm told."

Parker shrugged. "Let's say he's the *only* judge in the county."

"I can get a jury trial?"

"I suppose. I really don't know." Parker's face creased. "We haven't had any cases worse than drunk or disorderly. I'll look into it." Parker hesitated. "Your friends will be in court, don't worry."

"What about you, Sheriff?" Rosser asked. "Are *you* a friend?"

"I'm sheriff," Parker said bleakly and turned away.

16

ROSSER dozed fitfully through the night. He heard movement in the outer room, talk now and then but no one opened the door to his cell. He was awake early and saw the sun finally peek into his room. He was acutely hungry, but no one brought him anything to eat.

Finally, after an hour or more of the sun peeking into the room, the door was unlocked, Honsinger sang out, "Rise and shine, prisoner!" Then, "We're on our way to court and if things go right you'll be stretching rope before sundown."

Rosser got to his feet and walked past Honsinger, who stepped aside. "Outside, down the street — the new building that's gonna be The Great Plains Saloon. Judge's using it for a courtroom today."

Rosser left the marshal's office, with Honsinger following him closely. The street had only a few people on it. Rosser learned the reason as he approached the 'court' building. A crowd stood outside and there were at least fifty people inside.

The interior was still in process of being completed, but furnishings and lumber had been pushed aside. At the far end of the room a 'bench' had been made by planks being laid over sawhorses. Beyond the bench, on a nail keg, sat Judge Murcott. He was a frowsy-looking man of about forty-five, wearing a black frock coat, which looked as if it also served as a sleeping garment. He wore an unwashed shirt and had not shaved in several days. In his right hand he gripped a carpenter's hammer.

As Rosser and Honsinger approached, 'Judge' Morcott banged the hammer on the planks before him.

"Court is now in session," he announced. "Prisoner, do you plead guilty?"

"Guilty of what?" demanded Rosser.

"Oh, you're gonna give me a rough time, huh?" demanded Judge Morcott sourly.

"No, he ain't, Judge," said Johnny Honsinger. "I caught him in the act practically of killing Flon and that's all there's to it."

"Prisoner," snapped Judge Murcott, "let's get down to business. You heard the charge. Guilty or not guilty?" He poised his hammer, ready to bring it down on the planks in front of him.

Josh Moody pushed forward. "Wait a minute now. You're going too fast. Rosser's going to have a fair trial."

Murcott regarded Moody with a jaundiced eye. "You may be mayor of this here town, Josh, but I'm telling you, *I'm* the judge. I was elected by the people and you give me any trouble — "

Joe Leach and Doctor Kent stepped up beside Moody.

"Listen, Murcott," Doctor Kent said sardonically. "I don't know how you ever got elected judge of anything, but as long as you are judge, you're going to conduct yourself like one — "

"You're in contempt of court!" howled Murcott. "You can't talk to me like that."

"I can," said Doctor Kent firmly, "because I know you're a souse-pot and the next time you get the heebie-jeebies you can go and bag your head, instead of coming to me."

"You got no right to talk like that," whined Murcott, "not in front of people."

"Then pull yourself together and try to conduct a decent trial. A man's here on a serious charge and — "

"Nice speech, Doc," said Honsinger sarcastically. "Only it don't alter the facts. The prisoner killed a man — "

"Present your case," snapped Dr. Kent.

Honsinger regarded the doctor with smoldering eyes, then turned back to the judge. "Like I said, Judge. I heard these shots last night — "

"How many shots?" demanded Dr. Kent.

"Two–three."

"Two *or* three?"

"You his lawyer?" snarled Honsinger.

"No, but you're not a prosecuting attorney, either," retorted Dr. Kent. "You're the arresting officer, that's all."

Josh Moody said, "A man's on trial for his life. I think this should be a jury trial."

Riley Condor and Ken Rud, who had edged forward, confronted the mayor. "Jury trial suits us fine," said Condor. "Who'll pick the jury?"

Judge Murcott took his cue from Condor. "Yeah, you want a jury? I'll pick it for you."

"No, you won't!" shouted Josh Moody.

Murcott pointed the hammer at the mayor. "One more yip outta you, and I throw you out of here."

"You and who else?"

Honsinger faced the mayor. "Me,"

he said. "I'm the town marshal and I'll keep the peace. Go ahead, Judge, pick your jury."

"Never mind," said Rosser suddenly, "we'll do without the jury."

"You may be making a mistake," warned Dr. Kent.

"It's six of one, half a dozen of the other," Rosser said cynically, "if Murcott picks the jury."

Dr. Kent hesitated, then nodded. "All right, we'll proceed."

"Order in the court," shouted the judge. "Marshal, you was saying you come up right after the prisoner killed Mike Flon . . . "

A well-dressed man who had been standing just inside the door now came forward. "This is a farce. I've never seen a more ridiculous trial in my life . . . "

The judge stabbed at the newcomer with the hammer. "Who're you?"

"My name," the man said grimly, "is James Fenimore Fell."

A rumble went up in the courtroom.

Although his face was known to only two or three persons in the room, the name of the railroad builder was the most famous name in Montana.

Judge Murcott almost swallowed his Adam's apple.

"Uh — uh — Mr. Fell. It's a pleasure to meet you."

"I'm sorry I can't say the same about you," snapped Fell.

The judge turned very red, but the youthful marshal stepped into the breach. "Mr. Fell, you may be a big noise everywhere else, but right here you're just a man butting into something that ain't none of your business. You'll keep your mouth shut like everybody else or so help me, Mr. Big or Mr. Little, I'll throw you out of this goddam courtroom."

"That's telling him, Marshal!" cried out Riley Condor.

Jim Fell flinched almost as if he had been struck with a fist. Without another word, or even a glance at Tom Rosser, he turned and walked out of the room. A rumble went up in the crowd, which was silenced by Johnny Honsinger.

"Shut up, everybody. We got a man here to hang. Let's get down to business!"

His face cold with suppressed anger, Dr. Kent turned and faced the courtroom. "I'm getting sick and tired of a kill-crazy gunfighter pushing people around. If you people intend to stand for it — I don't."

"Doc," Honsinger said softly, "the devil's breathin' down your neck."

"I don't give a damn. I haven't got too long to live, anyway, and if I can do just one thing — "

"Easy, Doc," Riley Condor said suddenly. "We don't want more trouble than we already got. Marshal Honsinger, perhaps you'd better tone down your remarks . . . "

"Nobody steps on my toes," growled Honsinger. But he saw the attitude of his boss and suddenly shrugged. "Let's get on with this . . . "

"Christopher," Joe Leach said, "step up!"

The night hostler of the livery stable shuffled forward. "Chris," Leach continued, "you were on the job last night. Tell the court what happened. The truth — no more, no less."

"All I know," said the hostler, "I was sittin' in the stable when the big fellow — "

"What big fellow?"

"Flon. Like I said he come in and asked me what stall Alexander was in and when I told him he hit me one and I went out like a lantern. Next thing I knew there was a million people in the barn and somebody said Condor's name — "

"Objection!" howled Riley Condor. "I had nothing to do with Flon."

"He worked for you," snapped Dr. Kent.

"He did not. Oh, he hung around my place and he ran some errands for me once in a while, but I object to the insinuation that he was my man."

"Wasn't he your bodyguard?"

"I don't need a bodyguard."

"Then," said Dr. Kent deliberately, "everybody in Great Plains was fooled. Because everyone — and I repeat, *everyone* — believed he was your bodyguard."

"I can't help what people think," Condor said nastily. "For instance, everyone — and I repeat, *everyone* in town says that you're a drunken bum!"

Someone in the courtroom let out a guffaw, but it was not taken up by anyone else. Dr. Kent turned back to the hostler.

"All right, that'll be all. Rosser, I'd like to ask you a few questions."

"Go ahead."

"Why did you go to the livery stable last night?"

"Because a man came to the hotel and said I should go and take a look at my horse. The way he said it caused me to believe — "

"Never mind the *way* he said it. Who was the man?"

Rosser's eyes roamed across the spectators — picked out Guy Tavenner and beside him, Susan. Rosser shook his head.

"I didn't pay any attention to who it was."

Dr. Kent regarded him sharply. "Didn't you know the man?"

Rosser hesitated, then shook his head.

"Tom," Dr. Kent said earnestly, "I'm trying to establish that the whole thing was a trap — that Flon was *sent* to cut your horse's tendons and that another man was *sent* to tell you to go to the stable at the exact time, so you'd catch Flon in the act of crippling your horse."

"Doc," interrupted Riley Condor, "you been eating some of your opium pills."

Dr. Kent ignored the saloonkeeper. "The man who sent you to the stable, Tom . . . who was he?"

Rosser drew a deep breath, sent one covert glance at the taut-faced Susan

Tavenner and shook his head.

"I don't know . . . "

"*I* know!" rang out the voice of Susan Tavenner.

Guy Tavenner gasped. "Susan!" He reached savagely for her arm, but she eluded his grasp and started forward.

"It was my husband," she said firmly, then turned and pointed to Guy Tavenner. "I not only heard him tell Mr. Rosser to go and *look* at his horse, but I followed and I — I saw what happened."

A stunned silence fell upon the courtroom, then as a low murmur began to run through the spectators, Dr. Kent asked quickly, "What *did* you see, madam?"

"I saw that man" — pointing at the hostler — "lying on the floor unconscious and I heard the scream of Mr. Rosser's horse and then the — the big man came out of the stall. I saw the bloody knife in his hand." A shudder shook Susan Tavenner, but she went on, "I saw him coming toward

Mr. Rosser and then — then I heard the gun go off — and the big man fell to the floor."

"Damn you!" screamed Guy Tavenner. "Damn you for a meddling woman!"

"Thank you," cried Dr. Kent in a ringing voice. "Thank you for telling the truth, ma'am!" He whirled on Judge Murcott. "Still want to go on with this trial, Judge?"

The judge stared open mouthed at Dr. Kent. Then Sheriff Wes Parker came out of the crowd. "I can verify most of what Mrs. Tavenner just said. I arrived at the livery stable just as Flon came out of the stall and went for Rosser. I was a little too far away to see if Flon still had the knife in his hand, but there's one thing I want to point out, whether he had the knife or not. Flon's hands alone are lethal weapons. He's beaten some men in this town pretty badly. Crippled them. I believe Tom Rosser was fully justified in using his gun on Flon." He paused, drew a deep breath and added, "My recommendation — for what it is worth — is that Rosser be acquitted."

A sudden shout of approval went up in the courtroom. People surged forward. Judge Murcott saw what the overwhelming sentiment was and decided that discretion was his only hope.

He banged on the planks with his hammer and yelled, "Prisoner dismissed!"

17

ROSSER left the courtroom accompanied by Dr. Kent, Josh Moody and Joe Leach. Some attempt was made at conversation, but Rosser replied in monosyllables and the others soon fell silent.

At the hotel, Dr. Kent clapped Rosser on the shoulder. "Got to get back to my patients."

Rosser said, "Doctor, I know what you did for me. I'm not ungrateful, but there are things on my mind . . ."

"Sure," said Kent easily, "we'll get together some night and tie one on. Then you can tell me your troubles and I'll tell you mine."

He walked off quickly.

Josh Moody exclaimed, "The man saved your life, Rosser!"

"Yes," said Rosser, "with Mrs. Tavenner's help. Nothing much could have happened to Doctor Kent either way. Win or lose. But Mrs. Tavenner . . . "

"What could happen to her?" Moody asked cynically. "There's already trouble there." He smirked. "They have separate rooms now . . . "

Rosser gave him a quick look, fought down a sudden impulse and said stiffly: "Thank you, both of you . . . I'll see you later."

He turned and went off.

Moody and Leach exchanged glances. "Damn," said Leach. "How can you figure a man?"

"I think Doc hit it," Moody said thoughtfully. "He's got troubles. Big troubles." His eyes went to the hotel. "I wonder if Mrs. Tavenner is part of his trouble . . . "

The liveryman's eyes narrowed.

Rosser recrossed the street from the hotel and walked to the huge railroad building that would later be the depot for Great Plains. Several freight wagons stood in front of the building and a crew was unloading the wagons and stacking up crates of supplies and equipment on the ground in front of the building. Rosser had difficulty finding a passage that would lead him to the door and inside, but managed it after a few moments.

Inside, Bill Daves was checking a stack of flour sacks with the aid of a clerk.

"Rosser," he said, "heard about your trouble. Couldn't get to court myself, but I guess you got out of it all right."

"Not much," said Rosser. "I heard Mr. Fell's here."

Daves grimaced. "You, too? Everybody and his uncle'd like to see the Big Boss. He's tied up right now, but the way he snapped at me a while ago I doubt if he's in the mood to see anyone else."

"Ask him if I could have two minutes."

Daves frowned, glanced over his shoulder at a door. "You think we'd get

someone to act as a receptionist . . . "
He hesitated. "Wait until the young
lady comes out."

"Young lady?"

Daves closed one eye in a great
wink and then the door of Fell's office
opened and Susan Tavenner came out.
She was the last person in the world
Rosser would have expected to see at
this particular place, and it took him a
full second before he was able to move
forward.

"Mrs. Tavenner!"

She stopped, gave him a half-
frightened smile that froze instantly.

"I've got to talk to you," he said.

"Later," she murmured.

"At the hotel?"

She shook her head, was about to
speak, then Fell stepped out behind
her. Susan saw him, started forward.
"Yes," she said as she passed Rosser.

Fell was regarding Rosser as if he
had never seen him before.

"Mr. Fell," Rosser said, "I wonder
if I could talk to you for a minute."

Fell scowled, took out his watch and glanced at it. "I'm pretty busy, but" — he frowned, made an impatient gesture — "if it's not too long . . ."

He went into the office and Rosser followed. Fell closed the door, then gripped Rosser's hand. "I see you've been working." He shook his head. "That was pretty raw this morning."

"I made a mistake," Rosser said. "I should have killed the marshal."

Fell scowled. "That bad?"

"They've got the town sewed up and down and crosswise . . ."

"This man Fon — Flon . . ." Fell grimaced.

"Riley Condor's bodyguard. Condor built a frame-up, *wanted* me to kill Flon."

"His own man?"

"My guess is that he figured Flon had outlived his usefulness . . ." Rosser touched the bruises on his face.

Fell frowned and took a quick turn about the littered office, which had only two pieces of furniture, a desk made of rough lumber and a straight-backed chair. The rest of the room was piled high with cartons, boxes, crates.

Rosser watched him a moment. "There's something I think you ought to know. Certain citizens of this town are prepared to organize a vigilante committee . . . "

Fell wheeled, his mouth agape for an instant. Then his eyes blazed. "No!" he exclaimed. "Anything but that." A shudder seemed to shake him. "They still remember the Alder Gulch Vigilantes." He came up to Rosser. "You've got to stop it at all costs. Rather Condor and all his wolves — but not vigilantes . . . "

"They asked me to join . . . "

"You didn't?" Fell reached out, grasped Rosser's arm savagely.

"No, I feel much as you do about vigilantes — even if the men themselves are respectable." He grimaced. "In a way, *I'm* a one-way vigilante committee . . . "

"That's different!"

191

"Is it, Mr. Fell?"

"Stop the vigilantes, Rosser! I mean that . . ."

"To do that, I've got to stop Riley Condor and — "

"That's what you're here for, isn't it?"

"Yes." Rosser exhaled lightly. "Very well, Mr. Fell. When I took the job I gave you my word . . ."

"I'm holding you to that," Fell said grimly. He released Rosser's arm. "I don't care what you do — or how you do it — but no vigilantes. The newspapers back East would take that up quicker than anything else."

"I understand."

Rosser nodded, was about to turn back to the door when Fell exclaimed, "Wait! I'll be here for a week, but I don't think we should be seen together. If you must see me, come to my room at the hotel — Number Eight — but make sure no one sees you. Don't come here again during the day."

"I won't." Rosser touched the door,

then turned once more. "As I came in, Mr. Fell, a young woman left here . . . "

"What about her?"

"She helped me this morning. I'm afraid it's going to make trouble for her . . . "

Fell's eyes narrowed, then a faint smile crossed his stern face.

"She applied for a job." He waited for Rosser to ask the question, but when the town tamer did not, he said, "I was impressed with her sincerity, but a woman . . . here?"

"She might be very good," Rosser said.

Fell hesitated, then nodded. "She might at that. I think I'll take your suggestion." He took a slip of paper from his pocket, read from it. "Susan Tavenner . . . the hotel . . . " He said decisively, "I'll send a note to her — at once."

Rosser nodded and without another word, opened the door and went out.

Susan Tavenner inserted the key into the lock of her room but could not turn it. She jiggled the key back and forth then suddenly realized that the door was already unlocked. She gasped, was about to turn away, but the door was opened from inside and Guy Tavenner reached out and caught her arm.

He jerked her into the room, and as she fell forward he gave her a savage cuff on the side of the face. "You filthy wench," he swore. "I'll teach you to double-cross me!"

Susan had fallen forward against the bed, but recovered her balance and turned to face Tavenner as he advanced on her again. "Don't you dare," she cried, "don't you touch me again!"

"You mealymouthed hussy!" snarled Tavenner. "You fooled me with that Holy Hannah business. Sugar wouldn't melt in your mouth, don't touch me . . . and all the time you've been carrying on with another man."

"That's not true!" cried Susan.

"It was going on back in St. Paul,"

raged Tavenner. "It fits. The Sir Galahad business in the hotel lobby . . . and you were meeting him upstairs all the time."

Susan cried out in anguish and buried her face in her hands. "No, no, it isn't true."

"Separate rooms," mocked Guy Tavenner. "We had to have separate rooms when you came here. So you could meet him . . . " he lunged at her, caught her wrist and twisted it savagely. Susan let out a scream which Tom Rosser, coming up the stairs at that moment, heard.

He also heard the next words of Guy Tavenner as he strode swiftly up the hall.

"You're my wife, damn you," Tavenner shouted, "but if you want men on the side, I'll get them for you and they'll pay for their pleasure . . . "

That was as far as he got. Rosser slammed open the door, stepped in and caught Tavenner by a shoulder.

He whirled him around, smashed him in the face and, as Tavenner went limp, hurled him bodily out into the hall.

He followed, stooped and caught up the barely conscious Tavenner. Shaking him like a rat, Rosser said, "You touch her just once more, Tavenner, and I'll kill you. I'm not even going to warn you again. Understand?"

"D-don't," bleated Tavenner, "d-don't hit me again."

Rosser gave him one last contemptuous shove that again sent Tavenner sprawling. He managed to get up on his hands and knees and scuttled several feet down the hall before he picked himself up again and dived for the stairs, going down to the lobby.

Rosser turned back into Susan Tavenner's room. She was sitting on the edge of the bed trying to hold together the front of her dress, which Tavenner had ripped open.

"I'm sorry," Rosser said awkwardly.

"Please leave me alone," Susan cried miserably.

He winced, then realized that being caught in her predicament was possibly worse than the predicament itself. He backed out of the room. "I'll thank you later for this morning . . . "

He fled, passing his own room and going down to the lobby.

Tavenner had not wasted any time there. The hotel lobby was empty save for Josh Moody. The hotel man smiled grimly as he saw Rosser.

"Did I hear some noise upstairs?" he asked.

Rosser gave him a sharp glance, shook his head impatiently and headed for the door. Moody chuckled as Rosser went out.

18

AS Rosser stepped out of the hotel he automatically reached to tighten his trousers belt, then realized that he had eaten nothing since the day before. His eyes went across the street to Mary Donley's restaurant. It was midmorning and there should be few patrons.

He crossed diagonally and entered the restaurant. There were no customers at all and Mary, seated at the far end of the counter, doing some bookkeeping work, got up promptly.

She came forward, extending her hand. Rosser took it and nodded.

"Thanks."

"I should have let him have the other barrel," she said.

He shrugged and seated himself on the stool. Mary went behind the counter. "Anything you've got,"

Rosser said. "The marshal didn't want to waste breakfast on a man he figured would be hung."

"That Honsinger," Mary said, grimacing. "Him I can handle." She added thoughtfully, "Perhaps I will."

Rosser gave her a sharp, surprised look. She shook her head, smiled faintly. "You wouldn't think he had that much of a human streak in him."

"I'll admit I'm surprised."

"He only comes around late, after the customers are gone." Mary smiled, went to the kitchen and gave the cook orders for Rosser's breakfast. When she came back into the restaurant the sheriff was entering. He drew a Navy gun from under his belt, extended it to Rosser.

"Don't want to walk around without this."

It was Rosser's own gun appropriated the evening before by the marshal. Rosser nodded. "Appreciate your help this morning."

"Tavenner's wife did it," Parker said

briefly. He was quiet a moment. "Did you underestimate our marshal?"

"I *overestimated* him," said Rosser. "I didn't think he'd be quite as crude." He paused. "I guess he had his orders from Riley Condor."

"Condor," said Parker bleakly.

"You believe he set up the whole thing?"

"No question about it. Least not in my mind." Parker made a weary gesture. "A sheriff's pay is pretty good, but I made a living before I even wore a tin star. Least I got by."

"They wouldn't let you quit even if you wanted to," said Rosser, then added carefully, "would they?"

"Who'd stop me?"

"Honsinger?"

Parker frowned thoughtfully. "That's the trap a man gets into. Honsinger's got a reputation. You think about that and pretty soon you get to wondering." He grinned wanly. "Listen to me talk. You wore a badge for quite a few years."

Rosser nodded soberly. "I know what you're talking about. I guess that's the toughest part of it. You can't ever relax, let down for even a minute. Not even in your thinking . . . Rud been after you?"

"Rud?"

"You said he put your name on the slate."

"Yes," said Parker, "but he didn't put his brand on me when he did. I thought you would have known that."

"Sorry, Wes."

Parker nodded. "Don't blame you, after this morning. See you later." He left the restaurant.

Rosser looked at the door until Mary Donley spoke to him the second time.

"I said," she repeated, "that he wasn't the same kind as Honsinger."

"Parker thinks," said Rosser. "Honsinger doesn't. His reflexes react, that's all."

The Navy gun had been out of Rosser's hands for some hours and he was a careful man. He sat on his bed at the hotel late in the afternoon, with the moveable parts of the gun lying on the bed. He cleaned every piece, took off the old caps from the nipples and replaced them with new. He extracted the loads from the cylinder, reloaded them and was putting the last pieces of the weapon together when there was a timid knock on the door.

"Yes?"

"Mr. Rosser . . . "

Rosser sprang to his feet, crossed the small room and opened the door. Susan Tavenner, her face flushed a deep crimson stood in the doorway.

"I — I snapped at you," she said, embarrassed. "I want to apologize . . ."

"*You* apologize to me?" exclaimed Rosser. "After what you did for me this morning!"

Her eyes fell from his and she said hurriedly, "I just wanted to tell you that — that I've taken a position with the railroad."

"That's good," Rosser said.

"I — I've never worked before, but Mr. Fell was kind enough to give me this position and I'm going to do my best to — to support myself."

"Of course."

She started to turn away, hesitated, then with her eyes searching the area of the floor, she added, "I thought you might want to know . . . "

She fled then, going to her room beyond. Rosser stood out in the corridor, heard the key turn in her lock before he returned to his room. He slipped the Navy gun into the old holster, buckled it on and getting his coat, descended to the hotel lobby.

The clerk was on duty, but Josh Moody was just coming out of the dining room, picking his teeth with a gold toothpick.

"Just the man I want to see. Thought you might want a little relaxation tonight . . . same bunch."

Rosser shook his head. "Think I'll pass this one up. I might win another horse."

Moody sobered. "We wanted you on our side. I guess you know that."

"I *am* on your side," Rosser said. "Up to, but not including the vigilantes . . . "

"Forget that," said Moody easily. "Join us tonight."

"Just poker?"

"Draw and stud — nothing else," Moody smirked. "Lost a guest today. Tavenner moved out an hour ago. His room's already rented." Moody shook his head. "Town's filling up. Mr. Fell brought in a bunch of people. Now, if we can only — " He grimaced. "No, I won't get back on that subject."

Rosser nodded. "Perhaps I'll stop in for a while."

19

AS in Broken Lance, Kansas, Riley Condor had a back door to his office which led to an alley. About ten o'clock in the evening there was a careful knock on the door. Condor looked toward it, waited. The knock was repeated. He crossed to the door leading into the saloon, shot the bolt, then went to the alley door.

"Yes?" he called.

"Me," said a voice that Condor recognized.

Condor opened the door and Sheriff Wes Parker came in. He closed the door carefully, looked toward the front door. Condor made a small gesture. "Locked."

"You wanted to see me," said Parker heavily.

"Did I?"

There was a mocking note in

Condor's voice that was not lost on the sheriff, but he waited for Condor to speak again.

"I thought maybe you'd want to explain about this morning."

"What was there to explain?" asked Parker. "It was obvious that the woman's testimony had knocked the whole thing for a row of broken bottles. I figured best thing I could do was step in and try to make it *look* good."

"You made it look damn good," snapped Condor. "So good that I got to wondering if you'd forgotten who you are."

"I'm not likely to forget that, Condor," said Parker.

"Suppose you repeat it — just so I'm sure."

"Up to a point, Condor," Parker said heavily. "I'll take crowding up to a point. Don't go past that."

Condor knew that himself, but he was in an evil temper. "You're not indispensable," he snapped.

"I know I'm not. I found that out

today — yesterday rather, when you sent Flon to get killed."

"He was supposed to taunt Rosser into a fight, that's all."

Parker shook his head. "No," he said, "he was supposed to get killed."

"All right," snarled Condor. "He was a clumsy fool, and I've got no use for fools."

"Am I a fool, Condor?"

Condor made a tremendous effort to control himself. "This game's too big for us to quarrel."

"You're making the quarrel."

"I brought you here," Condor said heavily. "I had you elected sheriff and then I find you hobnobbing with my worst enemy, taking his side against me . . ."

"You had no side left this morning," said the sheriff. "The best thing I could do was what I did. He still thinks I'm his friend . . . and that's what you want isn't it?"

Condor glowered at the sheriff a moment. "You're sure he doesn't suspect who you really are?"

The sheriff hesitated, then shook his head.

Condor's eyes searched the face of the man before him . . . *the man who used the name of Wes Parker, but was really Lee Ring . . . the man from Idaho!*

20

MONEY was on the table before each of the five men; there was even money in the center of the table and poker hands had been dealt out, but no one had even looked at the cards. The men were Josh Moody, Joe Leach, Wendell Lewis, Dr. Norris Kent and Charlie Hodder.

Hodder, the banker, was saying, "The buzzards have got control, and we may as well face it — they intend to keep control. You had a sample today of what they'll do to anyone who dares to stand up to them."

"I've been thinking," said Josh Moody, "I'm the only town official who's not one of them. I believe I should resign . . . "

"No," said Wendell Lewis promptly, "there may come a time when we need *some* authority . . . "

"The sheriff isn't with them," the liveryman said. "Least, he came out for Rosser . . . "

"I'm not too sure," Dr. Kent said, frowning. "He's the one man I can't figure out."

"How about Rosser?" challenged Moody. Can you figure *him*?"

Dr. Kent hesitated, then nodded. "He's a loner. Ever since his trouble in Kansas."

"His trouble?" exclaimed Hodder.

"The woman he was going to marry got killed. The papers said that Rosser killed her himself, but I don't believe that."

"I hadn't heard about that," said Moody seriously. He looked around the ring of faces. "If there's something to that story, it may answer some questions about Rosser."

"Such as what?" asked Hodder.

"Why he hates Riley Condor."

"Riley Condor was in Broken Lance," Dr. Kent said thoughtfully. "Man I went to medical school with, Dr.

210

Masson, practices in Broken Lance. I think I'll write him a letter."

"Take you two weeks to get an answer," said Moody.

"We can't wait two weeks," declared Charlie Hodder. "Bank building will be ready day after tomorrow. Be damned if I want to open for business the way things are now."

Dr. Kent smiled frostily. "*My* business is better the way things are."

Wendell Lewis, the storekeeper, scowled. "My wife is coming out in two weeks. She's bringing our two children with her."

Josh Moody exclaimed, "We're beating around the bush, gentlemen. All of us know what's got to be done and — "

He broke off as a knock sounded on the door. All eyes went to the door, then returned to the poker table.

Dr. Kent picked up a ten-dollar gold piece. "I raised you ten, Charlie," he announced loudly.

"I call," said Hodder, just as loudly.

Moody stepped to the door and

opened it. "Rosser," he said, "glad you dropped in."

Rosser came into the room, nodded response to the greetings. "I'd like to sit in for a few rounds."

Dr. Kent kicked an empty chair, beside his own. "Right here, Tom." Then he winced, looked at his poker hand and tossed in the cards. "You win, Wendell."

Wendell Lewis blinked. "Eh?" Then he caught himself, laid down his cards and raked in the pot.

Rosser, about to sit down, decided to remain standing. "I guess you haven't really been playing . . . "

"If we haven't," exclaimed Dr. Kent, "then someone's stolen two hundred dollars from me." he picked up the partial deck at his elbow, raised it a few inches from the table, then dropped the cards, scattering them.

"No, Tom," he said, "we've only been pretending to play, in case you came in without knocking."

"That's what I thought." Rosser

drew a deep breath. "What's the verdict?"

"We want you on our side," the doctor said evenly.

"I *am* on your side."

"Josh," Dr. Kent said carefully, "you said you mentioned the vigilante thing to Tom."

"I did."

Rosser shook his head. "No."

"You won't join?"

"I'll repeat what I told Josh: I don't approve of vigilantes . . . "

"Even after what happened this morning? When you saw what kind of law we have in this town?"

"In spite of that."

Charlie Hodder said angrily, "Damn it, Rosser, what kind of a man are you?"

"I'm just what you see."

"That's no answer. You say you're with us, but then you say you're not. Make up your mind."

"Wait a minute, Charlie," interposed Dr. Kent. "We'll wind up calling each

213

other names. That may be a lot of satisfaction at the moment, but it solves no problems. Rosser, mind telling me why you came to Great Plains?"

"I've some land here . . ."

"There's land elsewhere."

"Doctor," Rosser said, "I owe you for what you did for me this morning. I haven't forgotten it. At the same time — " He stopped. The faces of the men around the table had become hostile. Even Dr. Kent's. "All right," Rosser went on, "I came because I heard that Riley Condor was here. I intend to kill him."

"Because of what he did in Broken Lance?" flashed Dr. Kent. "It was Condor who was responsible for the shooting of . . . Carol Grannan?"

A slow sigh escaped Rosser's lips. Without another word, he turned and left the room, leaving the door open.

Joe Leach began to swear, but was cut off by Josh Moody's gesturing hand, as he strode to the door. Moody looked out after Rosser, then drew back into the room. He closed the door, nodded.

"He's gone."

"You ask me," snapped Leach, "the man's lost his nerve."

"I don't think so," Dr. Kent said thoughtfully. "My lancet touched the injured nerve."

"One thing we can do," Hodder, the banker, said bitterly, "is write him off. Anything's going to be done has got to be done by . . . *us!*"

"It's time we got started," declared Wendell Lewis.

21

ROSSER stood in front of the hotel, looking down the street of Great Plains. There was plenty of light on the street from the lamps of the saloons. There was noise, the tinkling of a piano, singing and yelling. Somewhere, a gun was discharged. Rosser's eyes drifted to the door of the marshal's office. There was a light inside.

He drew a deep breath and exhaled. The men he had just left in Josh Moody's private room . . . they were crowding him. It wasn't the way to handle the situation, but he was being forced into it.

Fell was in Great Plains. Rosser felt sure that the railroad builder had his own sources of information and that he would learn of the formation of a Vigilante Committee the moment such a step was taken.

Rosser was forced to move, even though he knew the moment was not ripe. He let his hand drop lightly at his side to check that the leather thong that held down the bottom of his holster was securely tied. Then he stepped down from the veranda and started up the street. After a few yards he suddenly cut diagonally across the street.

He reached the sidewalk in front of the marshal's office, swerved a few feet to peer through the window, but as far as he could see, the office was deserted.

He continued on to Ken Rud's saloon and entered.

The place was doing a substantial business. A number of the customers, Rosser noted, seemed to be laborers. He threaded his way through the customers to the bar, where he was met by Ken Rud, who had seen him and come forward.

Rosser took a half dollar from his

pocket, tossed it to the bar. "Beer," he said to the bartender.

"Give him a short one," said Rud thinly.

"A regular," Rosser corrected, then to Rud: "Short?"

"Don't think you'll have time for a long one," Rud said sourly.

"I've got lots of time."

Rud shook his head angrily. "Do I have to spell it out for you? You're not welcome here."

Rosser sent a quick gesture about the room. "All these people get a personal invitation to come and spend their money here?"

The left side of Rud's face twitched as he tried to control himself. He said, "Rosser, if you're looking for trouble . . . "

The bartender set Rosser's glass of beer before him. Rosser picked it up, tasted a half mouthful and spat it out. "Stinking stuff," he growled, and tossed the glass to the bar.

The glass hit the bar, spilled the

beer and rolled on behind the bar, where it crashed to the floor. Rosser indicated the half dollar he had tossed to the bar.

"Take it out of that."

He turned to Rud, gave him an inquiring look, then walked deliberately out of the saloon. Rud stood without moving until the door swung behind him. Then he roared, "Blake!"

A swarthy man who was half Indian, or half Mexican, came swiftly from one of the faro games.

"Boss?"

"Damn you," swore Rud, "don't you ever watch what's going on in here?"

"Sure," was the swarthy man's reply, "somebody's beating Flannery's faro game and I thought — "

"Rosser was here," snarled Rud.

"Tom Rosser?"

"Is there any other Rosser in town?"

A furrow appeared on Blake's forehead. "Rosser's pretty tough . . . "

Rud reached into a vest pocket and brought out a coin, a ten-dollar gold piece. "Here's your pay," he said, and tossed the coin to Blake.

The man threw out his hand instinctively, caught the piece. "I got more pay comin' than that . . . "

"Get out!" said Rud ominously.

For one instant, Blake stiffened. Then he exhaled heavily, said, "All right," and headed for the door.

Next door to Rud's Saloon was Wendell Lewis's store. Beyond it was The Nugget, owned and operated by Councilman Harold Price, who weighed two hundred and twenty pounds, even though he stood but five feet six inches in his high-heeled boots.

He watched Tom Rosser as the latter came in and moved to the bar. He remained where he was, a good twenty feet from Rosser, as the bartender set out a foaming glass of beer. Rosser, in reaching for it, knocked over the glass.

Rosser's voice rose: "You clumsy oaf!"

"Mister," the bartender began, then yelled, "Lafe!"

Lafe was the lookout. He sat on a raised platform, overlooking two faro layouts. He heard the bartender's shout and stepped down from his perch.

He approached the bar as Harold Price finally came forward. Lafe gave his employer a quick glance, saw only bland impassiveness on his face and reached for Rosser.

"Mister," he began.

Rosser smashed him in the face. Lafe gasped, reeled back and bumped against Price, whose fat arms steadied him.

"Get him," said Price in a low voice.

Lafe stepped forward, then stopped. A shudder ran through him. "Rosser," he said thickly.

Rosser said savagely, "Don't ever make a move toward me again — if you want to live . . . "

"Lafe!" snapped the fat saloonkeeper. The tone of voice was a command, but Lafe remained still.

Rosser reached out, hit Lafe in the

face with the back of his hand, a contemptuous, stinging blow. Lafe took it with a shudder. Then Rosser finally fixed his gaze upon Price.

"You say something, fat man?"

Price said, "Get out of here!"

Rosser took a short step forward. His hand came up, raked Price's face with the knuckles. "My name's Rosser, *Mister* Rosser," he said. "See that you remember!"

Grinning mockingly, he made a half turn, started in an arc for the door. For most of the passage, he kept one eye on Price and his lookout man but finally, as he neared the door, he turned his back.

He stepped through the swinging doors unmolested.

Leaving The Nugget, Rosser stepped out into a dark doorway. His hand dropped lightly to the butt of his revolver.

The swinging doors of the saloon bulged outward and Rosser, watching, saw Lafe come out. He backed a few

222

inches deeper into the doorway, but Lafe did not look to the right or the left. He set out across the street.

Rosser came out of the doorway, gave a quick look toward the still swinging doors, then started to follow Lafe.

It was a short pursuit. Lafe crossed the street, went fifty feet and entered Riley Condor's Pleasure Palace. Not once had the lookout looked back and when he went through the doors, Rosser had closed up to within twenty feet of him.

As the biggest place in town, a stranger would have assumed that Riley Condor's establishment would have the largest attendance, but when Rosser stepped inside a quick glance around showed him that there were less than a dozen patrons.

At the rear, Condor stood in the doorway of his private office, talking to one of Ken Rud's bartenders. Lafe was bearing down on Condor.

Smiling wolfishly, Rosser stepped up

to the bar and said loudly, "Glass of beer!"

Riley Condor looked past Rud's bartender beyond Lafe, and saw Rosser. For one instant his face distorted angrily, but then it became cold, impassive. He came forward.

Sim Akins, seated at the table, suddenly got to his feet and also came toward the bar. There was a bright new star pinned to his flannel shirt. Rosser's eyes focused on it, but he addressed Condor, who was still a few feet distant.

"Mr. Condor," he said, "join me in a drink . . . "

"From what I've just heard, you don't need another drink," Condor retorted.

Rosser looked past Condor. Rud's bartender was watching him, open-mouthed. Lafe, Price's lookout, stood frozen. Rosser said, "Somebody talking about me?" Then without waiting for a reply, he whirled on Sim Akins.

"What's that on your chest?"

"It's a star," blustered Akins. "I just been made a deputy and — "

"Town's growing," Condor said tautly. "More trouble every day. Council figured our marshal needed help, so — "

Rosser pointed at Akins. "This the kind of scum this town likes for a marshal?"

"Rosser," Condor said heavily, "you're crowding — "

"Isn't that what you did yesterday?" Rosser taunted. "This morning . . . ?"

Condor sent a quick, desperate look about the saloon. His eyes returned fleetingly to Sim Akins then to Rosser.

"Get Honsinger," he said to Akins out of the side of his mouth.

"What for?" demanded Akins. "I can handle . . . "

Then his eyes met Rosser's and his face became wooden.

Rosser said, "Handle? Go ahead, handle me . . . "

Condor saw the sudden rigidness that had come over his former bouncer, made deputy marshal. He knew from old what happened to people when they confronted Tom Rosser, when the eyes of Rosser burned into them, when the death challenge was hurled at them. Only one man, in Condor's experience, had never actually backed down before the former marshal. No, two, counting Johnny Honsinger.

But neither Honsinger, nor the other man . . . *the man from Idaho* . . . was here at the moment.

Condor said thickly, "Another time, Rosser . . . "

Rosser knew that every man in the saloon was watching, listening. Though sparsely patronized there were still enough men here who would carry the story through Great Plains.

He brought up his hand and, as he had done to Harold Price, raked the back of it across Condor's face. A rough, bruising, backhanded blow. But it was not the pain of it that did the harm. It was the contempt, the studied deliberateness of it.

A hush was upon the Pleasure Palace and every man in it heard Condor's words, heard them, even though they came almost as a whisper.

Condor said, *"You'll get this back, Rosser, you'll get it back, like you got it in Broken Lance . . ."*

Rosser hit him again. This time his hand was closed into a fist.

ROSSER stood in the shadows of the hotel veranda and watched the street of Great Plains. A half hour ago there had been light and noise, but most of it from inside the saloons. Very few people had been abroad. Now there was activity on the street.

A man came running along, headed across the street, into the marshal's office. A moment later, two men came out, ran down the street, and then cut across to the Pleasure Palace. A third man came out of the marshal's office.

Another runner went pell-mell into The Nugget. One raced to the saloon of Ken Rud. Then, suddenly, a large section of Great Plains's population seemed to be abroad. Men poured out of saloons, other men entered the saloons. There was running up the street, down the street, galloping of horses' hoofs. A gun banged on the street. A moment later there was a muffled report from inside one of the saloons.

Yet no one came to the hotel. Rosser stood in the shadows ten minutes, fifteen.

There was a step inside the hotel and Rosser, turning, saw Wendell Lewis coming out. Lewis did not see him. Another minute went by and Joe Leach came out. The 'poker game' was breaking up. Rosser made a mental note that it had lasted until now, a full half hour, after he had himself left the room.

Voices from inside the lobby came to Rosser and then Charlie Hodder and Dr. Kent appeared. They stepped onto the veranda.

Hodder said, "You're the logical one for the job, Doc. They heard you this morning and they'll follow you."

"I'm not too sure," Dr. Kent replied.

"They know I defended Rosser and they'll think — "

His words broke off abruptly, as he saw Rosser in the shadows only a few feet away.

Rosser said, "Evening . . . "

"Rosser," exclaimed Hodder. "Be damned . . . !"

"We were just talking about you," Dr. Kent said testily.

"I know. I was going to stop you. Cough, or something . . . "

"Well?" snapped the banker.

"I didn't hear enough," said Rosser. His voice spoke a little louder. "Of course, I can guess!"

"Don't," said Dr. Kent, "don't guess!"

"Good night," Rosser said evenly. He came forward, to the door.

"Night," the banker snapped.

"See you tomorrow," Dr. Kent said in a strained voice.

They stepped down from the veranda and Rosser reached for the hotel door. It was then that the footsteps came toward the hotel. They were heavy footsteps, but even in pace.

Rosser stepped quickly aside from the door.

Dr. Kent and Hodder had started across the street, so the newcomer was not seen by them and did not have to greet them. He came into sight.

Sheriff Wes Parker.

He stopped at the veranda steps. He was a careful man. He had seen men leaving the hotel veranda, might even, at the distance, have made out a third shadowy figure.

Rosser spoke: "Wes . . . evening . . . "

The sheriff climbed the short flight of stairs. "Thought you might be here," he said.

"I was just going inside," Rosser said. "I waited, but — "

"It won't be tonight."

"Honsinger isn't around?"

"Oh, yes, he showed up." Parker grunted. "He was taking a nap in the office. Lost sleep last night, I guess . . . " The sheriff paused carefully. "You raised some hell!"

"They've always told me that every man's entitled to a little hell-raising."

"Surprised me. I somehow didn't think" — the sherriff's nostrils sniffed audibly, then added in some slight surprise — "you're sober . . . !"

"I had about two mouthfuls of beer."

"Condor said you were drunk. So did Price and Rud."

"The clan's gotten together," Rosser noted. "Figured they would."

"Oh, sure. Condor thinks his jaw is broken."

"Hope so."

"Honsinger was ready for the showdown. Condor talked him out of it."

"His jaw can't be broken, then . . . I didn't think he'd hold Honsinger back."

"Didn't think so myself, but I guess it was the right thing to do. Town knows about the trial this morning. Honsinger didn't come off good. Neither did Condor. You've got public sympathy." Parker paused. "I said, *public* sympathy."

"I heard it."

"The drinking part of it. People saw it and everybody figures you had a right to get drunk and do a little slapping around. Condors knows that. But he knows, too, that you did it at Rud's, then at Prices's before you came to him. He knows you did it deliberately, but he's going to take the drunk stand. For a while."

Rosser was quiet. The sheriff said, after a moment, "My hunch is that Condor can hold Honsinger back only up to a point. There's something in the man I'm just beginning to figure out. A wolf I ran into over in — up in the mountains. He was mad. Went for my horse, then at me. Two bullets to stop him. Honsinger's like that. He's got something in that head of his . . . something that makes him *want* to kill."

Rosser said, "Perhaps I've underestimated him. He's right with me every minute. Ahead of me, at times . . ."

"Honsinger?" asked the sheriff. Then grunted: "You weren't even listening."

"I'm sorry," said Rosser. "I heard you, but — I was thinking of Condor."

"In your place, Tom, I'd *keep* thinking of him. Don't stop for one minute. Tonight . . . well, tonight may be all right, but tomorrow . . . and the day after . . . "

"Thanks, Wes . . . Sheriff . . . "

Parker raised his hand in a half salute. "'Night."

He turned and stepped down from the veranda. Rosser watched him a moment, then turned into the hotel.

Inside the lobby, Rosser came to an abrupt halt. Across the room, seated in an armchair, was James Fenimore Fell. He was scowling at a sheaf of papers in his hand.

Bill Daves was at the desk talking earnestly in low tones to Josh Moody. It was Moody who saw Rosser.

"Mr. Rosser," he said loudly.

Bill Daves whirled. "Uh — Mr. Rosser," he said.

234

It was obvious to Rosser that the two men had been discussing him. He nodded, continued on toward the stairs. Then Jim Fell looked up.

"Mr.Rosser!"

Daves, hearing his master's voice, started across the room. "Mr.Fell, this is Mr . . . "

"We've met," Fell snaped. "This afternoon — since you've forgotten."

Daves grimaced, turned and went back to the hotel desk.

Rosser crossed to Fell. The latter gestured to a straight-backed chair beside him. "Sit down."

Rosser took the chair. Fell gave a last scowl at the papers in his hand, shook his head. "I've thought over that matter we discussed this afternoon, Rosser. I've decided against it."

Rosser nodded. "Very well, sir," he said in his normal tone of voice.

Fell said, low, "I wormed it out of Daves. There *is* a vigilante movement. Who's behind it?"

"Talk to Daves again," Rosser said.

Fell gave a low exclamation. "Damn it, I asked him outright and he denied he was any part of it. Who else?"

Rosser's eyes flicked across the hotel lobby to Moody and Daves. They were talking again, but the eyes of both men were furtively watching Rosser and Fell.

"The mayor," grunted Fell. "It's worse than I thought." His voice became loud again, gruff. "Very well, I'll think about it. Come and see me in a day or two."

Rosser rose. "Good night, sir!"

He turned to the steps, ascended.

There was light in the upper hallway. Two lights, one at each end.

There had been only one light in Broken Lance.

23

ROSSER lay on his bed in the darkness. He was fully dressed except for his coat. His hands were linked under his head and his eyes were open.

It was a half hour since he had come to his room, but sleep would not come. Not even physical fatigue. There was no shaking of the hand, tremor of the limbs; he had tested that upon first entering the room.

Killing was his business, killing and strife. It wasn't those things that caused him to sometimes shake. It was . . .

Footsteps sounded in the hall. Rosser heard them as they came from the steps onto the uncarpeted floor of the second floor. He followed the steps to his room.

There was a peremptory knock on the door.

In one single movement, Rosser's feet swing to the floor, propelled himself up and to one side.

"Yes?" he called, his hand whipping up the Navy gun.

"Rosser?" asked a voice outside.

"Come," Rosser replied.

The doorknob turned and Jim Fell stepped forward. He saw the gun in Rosser's hand. "Don't you lock your door?" he demanded.

"I trust my ears more than the lock," Rosser replied. He dropped the revolver into his holster. Fell swung the door shut, looked and saw the only chair in the room.

"I've a good notion to build a hotel," he snapped as he seated himself. "My room's the same as this."

"I imagine they're all the same," Tosser replied. "I guess Moody never thought you'd be staying here."

"Moody," grunted Fell. "The mayor. Their leader . . . "

"I don't think so," said Rosser. "He may have started as the leader, but I think they've shifted to Dr. Kent."

"I don't know him."

"He's the man defended me in court . . . "

"The kangaroo trial," Fell nodded. "He's a good man?"

"He's dying of t.b. . . . "

Fell scowled. "Would have to be a man like that. Doesn't give a damn about life himself."

"He cared about me, Mr. Fell!"

Fell made an impatient gesture. "Later about that. Man came into the hotel right after you went upstairs. Veach, Leach . . . "

"Joe Leach."

Fell nodded. "He talked loud. Couldn't help but hear him." Fell's eyes sought Rosser's. "True?"

"What?"

"He said it happened only a little while ago."

Rosser nodded. "Yes."

"You went from saloon to saloon deliberately trying to pick a fight."

"Isn't that why I'm here?"

"I heard some names mentioned. Rud." Fell's eyes seemed to be boring into Rosser's. "And Riley Condor . . ."

"Yes," said Rosser.

"I remembered the name from St. Paul. He's the reason you took the job."

"They've a syndicate," Rosser said evenly. "The syndicate held the town elections, put up the candidates and voted them into office."

"Moody, the mayor?"

"He's the dummy, the front man. He has *this* much authority." Rosser snapped his fingers.

"That why he's talking up the vigilantes?"

"No, I don't think so."

"Riley Condor," Fell said abruptly.

"He heads the syndicate."

"Leach said you slapped his face."

"There was a little more than that."

"I can read between the lines. But *did* you slap his face?"

Rosser nodded.

A grim smile came over the railroadman's face. "A slap in the face, to some people, can be worse than a blow on the head with a brick. I take it Condor's that kind of man?"

"There were customers who saw it . . . and some of his own people."

"They didn't defend him?"

"No." Rosser paused, then added, "Condor gives the orders."

Fell got to his feet. "Good enough. You'll be getting action, I imagine. Pretty soon."

He stepped to the door. Rosser said, "The vigilantes . . . "

Fell shook his head. "By the time they get organized . . . "

It was on Rosser's tongue to tell him that the vigilante organization was already formed, but Fell was opening the door and Rosser let him go.

This time, Rosser shot the bolt. He unbuckled his gunbelt, hung it from the bedpost and took off his boots.

He slept, after a while.

24

SUSAN TAVENNER also slept. It was the first sound, restful sleep she had had in more than six weeks. She had crossed her personal Rubicon. Guy Tavenner was no longer in her life.

In her own mind, Susan was free. She had obtained a position and would be able to take care of herself. Although — and the thought was comforting — she had made the decision *before* she had gotten the job with the railroad.

She slept and in the morning made her toilette and descended to the hotel lobby shortly after six o'clock. The night clerk yawned from behind the desk, then exclaimed. "It's only ten minutes after six!"

Susan indicated the dining room. "They're serving breakfast, I believe."

"Sure, the working people get up early."

"What time do the *working* people start work?"

"Seven o'clock, but . . . "

"I," said Susan, "am a working person." She walked into the dining room.

Jim Fell, at a table near the door, was raising a forkful of pancake to his mouth. He lowered it to his plate.

"You're going to work this early?" he asked.

"Isn't seven o'clock the proper time?"

Fell got to his feet and indicated the chair across from him. "It is. Won't you join me?"

Susan held back a moment, then realized that she could do no less. She seated herself opposite Fell.

"I'm late," Fell said. "In St. Paul I begin at six o'clock." He smiled frostily. "I do not expect the employees to report that early, however."

"I am willing to do whatever is necessary," Susan said evenly.

243

"I'm sure you are." Fell relaxed. "As a matter of fact, I can use your services early this morning. About a hundred men came here yesterday. Freighters, graders, tracklayers. They've been promised some pay and I brought the money with me. They'll be lining up even now, if I know my people . . . and I think I do. Daves would be all day paying them. He'll be glad of your help."

And so, a half hour later, Susan found herself seated beside Bill Daves at a plank table, counting out money. Daves accepted the work slips from the workers as they shuffled forward, made rapid estimates: "O'Hara, thirty days, sixty dollars, Callahan forty days, sixty dollars," and Susan counted out the money from stacks of coin and handed it to the horny-handed tracklayers, teamsters, roustabouts.

The paying of the men was completed by ten o'clock; by that time those who had been early in line had already squandered part of their pay. The saloonkeepers who had been closing anywhere between two and four o'clock in the morning and reopening sometime between eight in the morning and noon had somehow gotten wind of the payday and were ready to receive the railroadmen.

Faro and poker games were going strong by ten o'clock. A full complement of bartenders were serving drinks and the gamblers were bright-eyed and smooth-fingered.

At eleven o'clock, a freighter reeled out of the Pleasure Palace Saloon, searched his pockets and found that the month's pay he had had in his pocket two hours ago was gone. But the whiskey was warm within him and he staggered across the street and by his sense of smell found the door of Ken Rud's saloon.

A score of railroad men were inside and the man without money was soon adding liquid warmth to what he already had in his stomach.

By twelve o'clock there were a dozen

or more men with empty pockets. Three freighters then found themselves rebuffed by a half dozen tracklayers and graders when they tried to get in on the rounds of drinks. A fight ensued. The freighters gave a good account of themselves, but were losing when a pair of Rud's strong-arm men joined in the fray and rushed the freighters out of the saloon.

They went to Harold Price's Nugget and found a half-dozen freighters who still had some pay left.

At twelve-thirty, a grader put his last silver dollar on the faro layout in Fred Wagoner's salon. The dealer swooped in the coin, and said, "Ten wins, Jack loses. If you're not playing, mister, step back."

The grader was only fighting drunk. He snarled, "You got all my money. I got a right to watch my friends lose theirs . . ."

The dealer made a swift movement toward his vest. A double-barreled derringer appeared in his hand. "I said make room for the cash customers."

The grader stared at the gun a moment, then without a word turned and walked off. One or two railroad men followed him, but their places were quickly taken by others, eager to lose their money.

Rosser did not leave the hotel until eight o'clock, although he had been awake for some time before. He was halfway across the street before he became aware of the unusual activity, due to the influx of Fell's railroad workers.

Even Mary Donley was receiving some benefit from the railroad men, for there were some workers who thought food more important than drink. Or perhaps they were of the opinion that a base of food was necessary for the later drinking.

A grader was just leaving a stool as Rosser stepped into the restaurant. It was the only vacant seat in the place and Rosser slipped into it. Mary

Donley was clearing away the dishes before Rosser had seated himself.

"I heard," she said. "It's all over town. About last night . . ."

"When I was a marshal," Rosser said, repeating himself, "they always told me every man was entitled to get drunk once in a while . . ."

"Were you? Were you drunk?"

He looked her steadily in the eye and shook his head.

"I didn't think so," she said.

"Pancakes and aigs," sang out the voice of the cook through the food slot.

Mary frowned. "Busiest day we've ever had . . ."

She went off and Rosser looked around the restaurant. Dr. Kent, at a table with three railroad men, gave him a mocking half-salute. Two minutes later the stool beside Rosser was vacated. There were two waiting customers, but Dr. Kent got up from his table, and coming forward, dropped onto the stool beside Rosser.

"Sometimes," he said to Rosser, "I run into a man I can't make out. You wouldn't play *poker* with us last night, but then you went out and stood Condor on his ear."

"Not on his ear," said Rosser.

Kent grinned sardonically. "Allowing for some exaggeration, it was quite a stunt. I'd have paid a hundred dollars to have seen it."

"Doctor," Ross said, "you say you sometimes can't figure a man. I might say the same about you. You talk hard, but when the chips are down, you're a pretty respectable citizen."

"Up to a point," Dr. Kent said.

"A high point," Rosser said. "*I* know how high."

For a brief moment, Dr. Kent's face became serious. He stared at Rosser, started to say something, then changed his mind and rose. His hand clapped Rosser's shoulder and he went out of the restaurant. Rosser noted that he did not pay for his meal. He had forgotten. Or perhaps he paid by the week.

Mary's restaurant was still crowded when Rosser finished his breakfast, customers having come in to take the places of those who left. Rosser was pleased that Mary's business should prosper and knew that no matter what happened in Great Plains in the next few days her future was secure.

She would not need Johnny Honsinger, or men of his kind.

Or Rosser.

Rosser recrossed to the hotel and stood for a while on the veranda, watching the unusual traffic on the street. His eyes drifted to the livery stable.

After a moment he shook his head impatiently. He stepped down from the veranda, walked steadily across the street.

A day hostler was helping Joe Leach unload a wagonful of grain. Leach, gripping a heavy sack, saw Rosser. He carried the sack six feet to a pile, deposited it and nodded to Rosser.

"Mr. Rosser!"

Rosser said evenly, "I would like a horse."

Without hesitation, Leach replied, "Of course, Mr. Rosser."

Rosser was aware of the 'Mister,' but let it pass. Five minutes later he was riding out of great Plains.

The horse under Rosser was a good one, but it was not Alexander. Rosser forced himself to think of something he had heard years ago; no man should become attached to a horse or a dog. A horse was a means of transportation, a dog should be used to guard property. They should never become pets or friends.

And no man, Rosser told himself should become too attached to another person.

Well, perhaps there could be exceptions. People who lived in civilized communities, who were engaged in normal pursuits of life. Men who worked for a living with their hands, who had wives, families and homes.

Not men who were employed as town tamers.

No man who was a town tamer had a right to think of a future life, of a woman.

Not a woman like Carol Grannan, or . . . Susan Tavenner.

25

YET, Rosser continued on the tract of land that was his by right of the deed in his pocket. He rode through the lush grass that would feed many fine horses. He stood on the knoll overlooking the stream and finally he turned his horse and started it upward, toward the timberland that could be used for building purposes, for fuel, shelter for livestock.

The sun flashed on metal, at the edge of the timber. Rosser, by instinct alone, threw himself sideways. The whine of a bullet reached his ears before the bark of the rifle, a split second later. Rosser's gun was in his hands but even as he pulled the trigger he knew that the range was too great for a revolver, that the other man had a rifle, and thus the advantage.

Bent low over the saddle, with most

of his body on the right side, Indian fashion, Rosser sent the horse into a terrific gallop paralleling the timber.

From under the horse's neck, Rosser saw the small puff of smoke as the hidden rifleman fired a second time. The bullet missed the back of the horse by a fraction of an inch.

Rosser turned the horse, head on for the trees, thus offering a smaller target to the rifleman.

It caused the man to lose his nerve. Instead of firing a third time he clambered onto a horse and burst into the open, away from Rosser.

Rosser shot erect in the saddle, for he knew that the rifleman's accuracy, shooting backwards from a galloping horse, would be negligible. It would be a straight pursuit, a ride-down.

But that, Rosser knew within moments, was not to be. The animal under him was an ordinary one, a livery stable for-hire hack.

The horse ahead was a range animal, used by a rider accustomed to hard and swift rides. In a hundred yards, Rosser's mount lost twenty feet. Rosser kept on for another hundred yards merely to force the rider ahead to continue his flight, but then he pulled up the already heaving animal.

Condor was drawing the noose about Rosser. He knew of the latter's land, knew that he came out to it and had staked out an assassin. What happened here would not have to be explained. Especially if there was no body to explain away.

Rosser, from here on, would be contained within the confines of Great Plains. He rode back into the town.

Joe Leach was not in the stable when he dismounted. The hostler came to take the horse.

"Be a dollar," he said.

Rosser knew that the man had received his instructions. Rosser was to be treated as any customer, on a cash basis. It was the way Rosser wanted it. He gave the man a dollar, clapped the horse on the flank and went out upon the street.

He started for the hotel, changed his mind and strolled to the railroad depot. The last stragglers were moving slowly into the depot, where they received their pay.

Rosser glanced inside, saw Susan counting out money, and shaking his head, turned away.

By three o'clock in the afternoon, fifty percent of the newly paid railroad workers were drunk. Some had passed out in the saloons, were being permitted to sleep it off, their heads resting on tables. Some had gone to the alleys behind the saloons, under their own power, or dragged or propelled there by the saloons' bouncers.

At least a dozen sat in doorways too stupefied to move. A few were lying in them, unconscious, and still another few had collapsed on the sidewalks. Two lay out in the street and traffic flowed around them.

Another twenty-five per cent could

not be classified as 'drunk,' for they still possessed powers of locomotion. Perhaps ten per cent of the remainder had vast capacities for whiskey and were still engaged in putting it away.

Less than five percent of the railroad men had not taken a single drink. They were the rare few that are found everywhere, teetotalers, or men who sent their pay home to families in the East.

That left another ten per cent who drank, but were cautious about it.

The trouble started among these ten per cent. Most of them were gamblers and they drank carefully, perhaps, for that reason. They wanted their faculties unimpaired. Even in a crowd of a dozen there are troublemakers. Among one hundred and twelve men there are bound to be at least ten troublemakers.

One of these knocked over a faro table in Ken Rud's saloon. He was knocked unconscious by a blow on the head dealt by Rud's lookout. Two of his friends, who came to his assistance, suffered scalp lacerations and assorted bruises before they were dragged out to the alley and thrown down within a few feet of a couple of plain drunks.

In the Pleasure Palace, another troublemaker grabbed up Guy Tavenner's faro box and smashed it open, revealing certain hidden mechanisms that were standard for many faro dealers, but were frowned upon by players.

Tavenner shot the troublemaker through the right arm. The man had only one friend with him, and this man was clubbed by Sim Akins with the long barrel of his frontier model. When he recovered consciousness he found himself on the ground, in the alley.

26

ROSSER sat on the veranda of the hotel and watched the hustle and bustle of the busy afternoon. Marshal Johnny Honsinger and his new deputy, Sim Akins, were doing a thriving business. Singly, and in pairs, they herded troublemaking railroad men into the jail. One they dragged along the sidewalk and another Sim Akins brought in on his back.

Several bleeding carousers staggered or were led or carried into Dr. Kent's office.

It was not an unusual sight to Tom Rosser. He had been in the Kansas trail towns when cattlemen paid off their trail hands. The men acted like — like the railroad workers, given a month or two months pay. They got drunk, they gambled and they fought. In those days, Rosser, as a marshal himself, had been compelled to arrest men. In that respect, Marshal Honsinger and Deputy Akins were performing proper duties.

It did seem to Rosser that there were too many bloody faces and heads among those that were going into the jail, but that was merely a matter of personal opinion. There had been rough marshals in the trail towns. The famous Wyatt Earp had preferred to 'buffalo' his arrestees, said buffaloing consisting of laying the barrel of a Frontier Model along the side of a man's face. With force.

It was nearing four o'clock when Rosser became aware of the growing crowd across the street in front of the doctor's office, and next door to the jail. First there were only three or four railroad workers, then in a little while the crowd grew to seven or eight, and finally to a dozen or more.

There was milling in the crowd, growing talk. Little yelling, but much gesticulating. There was even a leader who finally became separated from the others by turning his back to Dr. Kent's office and haranguing the group.

The man's name was Kevin; he was foreman of a tracklaying gang and stood about six feet six inches. He had fiery red hair and a temper that seemed to match his head thatch.

"I've been up and down the street," he was saying passionately. "I haven't found six of our boys with a dollar left in their pockets. They couldn't have spent all that money on the rotgut that's been swilled today. Most of it's been taken from them — stolen by the crooks and card sharps in every dive along this street . . ."

"McClosky lost his whole poke in twenty minutes," shouted one of the railroad men. "You couldn't lose money that fast in an honest game."

"I put in my time on the Northern Pacific," another man growled, "and I worked on the Katy and the Santa Fe. I've seen smooth-fingered bastards in every railhead town for fifteen years. I never saw a bunch as slippery, or as raw, as what I've seen today in this here Great Plains."

"That's what I'm trying to tell you," snarled the foreman of the tracklayers. "I don't play faro myself because of the damn crooked boxes the dealers always use, but I lost my roll playing poker. I got four kings dealt to me and the houseman showed four aces. That ain't decent."

"Same thing happened to me," shouted another man. "On'y I had a straight flush and the crook beat me with a royal flush. No man can get a royal flush more'n once in a lifetime, but damned if I didn't see four of them today at Riley Condor's place . . . all four by the same dealer!"

"Riley Condor skinned me in Kansas," snapped the foreman Kevin. "He drew a royal flush on me in Trinidad, Colorado, six years ago that I know damn well he brought out of his sleeve . . . " He gripped his left shoulder with his right hand. "He put a forty-one slug into me when I swung on him."

"Let's take this damn town apart," roared a man in the crowd.

It was a popular suggestion and a wild yell went up. Rosser, watching from across the street, saw the crowd surge up the street. It passed Ken Rud's Saloon, shifted to the left and bore down upon the Pleasure Palace.

The crowd inside the Pleasure Palace had thinned out. Only a few railroad men had money left. Riley Condor, carrying an open cashbox, was collecting money from one of the faro games when Kevin and his dozen or more railroad men stormed into the big saloon.

Condor gave a quick signal to a bouncer. A command was flung across the room and three men, all armed, one of them with a short-barreled shotgun, converged and blocked the mob from the table section of the room. A Condor cohort darted into

263

Condor's private office and went out through the alley.

Kevin signaled to his followers to stop. He confronted the three armed Condor men.

"We aim," Kevin said, "to get back half of the money that was taken from us today. I say *half* because we was drunk and I figure we ought to pay something for the booze." He thrust out a grimy hand. "I lost ninety-six dollars in here. I want forty-eight dollars . . ."

"Get out," said the Condor man with the shotgun. "We've had enough trouble with you people today."

"Trouble?" snapped Kevin. "You don't know what trouble is. Not yet . . . and if you point that bird-gun at me, I'll take it away from you and ram it down your throat!"

Condor had closed and put down his cashbox. He came forward.

"Mister," he said savagely, "you've had your drinking and you've had your fun . . ."

Kevin shot a quick look over his shoulder. "There's thirteen–fourteen of us here. We figure we got fifty dollars apiece coming, give or take a few cartwheels. We want that money, or we wreck the place."

The man in front of Kevin now did point the muzzle of the shotgun at the railroad foreman. Kevin, keeping his eyes on Condor, made a movement toward him, then pivoted and grabbed the shotgun out of the man's hands.

"I told you what I'd do to you with this gun," he began. He raised the shotgun over his head like a harpoon, with the muzzle forward and downward.

Riley Condor's short-barreled .44 came out from under his coat, spat fire and thunder. The bullet went into Kevin's stomach. Kevin folded forward, gasping . . . but the gun muzzle went down and smashed into the former gun wielder's mouth. Unfortunately the man had his mouth closed, so the muzzle could not go down his throat. But it broke most of his teeth and chin.

The man let out an unearthly cry of anguish as he reeled backwards.

The scream drowned the report of Condor's second shot. Kevin went to his knees. Even then, with two bullets in him, he lunged toward Condor. His huge hands clawed at his legs. Deliberately, Condor thrust down his revolver and sent a bullet into the back of the already dying man's head.

The railroad men were stunned. Only momentarily, for the two Condor men, inspired by the performance of their employer, now suddenly opened fire.

There were an odd dozen of men before them. They could not miss. Bullets slammed into bodies, tore through vitals. They thudded and whacked, smashed bones and bore deep into flesh.

The Condor men continued to fire even when the mob melted before them. The railroad men hit the batwing doors, almost tearing them from their hinges. Left behind were three dead men, Kevin and two others . . . And three men who did not move, but were alive.

A railroad man who had not been part of the mob because he still had a few dollars left that he had been trying to lose in Guy Tavenner's faro game, came forward, saw the shambles and cried out in awe, "Holy Mother of God!"

One of the Condor men pointed his gun at him, pulled the trigger. But there was only a click for the gun was empty.

"Beat it," said Riley Condor thickly.

The railroad man ran toward the door. A yard from it he stopped, shot one terrible look back upon the scene, then stumbled through the door.

Riley Condor whirled on his two hirelings. "You stupid, stupid bastards!" he raged.

"We on'y done what you done," whined one of the men.

Condor raised his gun in which there

still three bullets. But the tiny spark of self-preservation that was always so present in him kept him from firing.

He sent a slow look about the room. Three bartenders were looking on in awe, five gamblers and dealers, two patrons who were railroad men, but too far bemused by whiskey to really know what happened, and four or five other customers, who were older Great Plains residents.

Witnesses.

Condor let out a low groan. Then he became alert. Marshal Johnny Honsinger, summoned by the Condor man who had gone out through the alley door, burst in from the same direction. Close on his heels was Deputy Sim Akins.

They came into the saloon.

"Christ," said Honsinger, when he saw the dead and wounded.

Sim Akins whistled.

"They tried to take the place apart," said Riley Condor. "We — we had to defend ourselves."

Honsinger walked among the remnants of the recent carnage. He thrust at one of the men with his boot. "This one's still peepin', but not for long." He counted. "Three for sure, one soon . . . " He came to the man, sitting with his back against the bar, his hands clawing at his stomach.

"How you feel?" he asked the man brutally.

The man's mouth worked as he tried to speak and could not. Blood frothed on his mouth, then shot from it in a stream. The man fell over sidewards.

"Five," Honsinger counted.

He saw a man who lay on his side, both hands gripping his left knee.

"Customer for the doc," he called to Sim Akins.

Akins came forward. His face was white, his lips trembling. "Jeez," he said. Then: "There's gonna be hell to pay for this."

Johnny Honsinger chuckled wickedly.

269

"This town *is* hell!" He looked at Riley Condor. "Eh?"

"Get them out," snapped Condor.

"Not my job," Honsinger retorted. "Not the dead ones. Have your own boys tote them off."

27

ROSSER had watched the formation of the railroad mob across the street from the hotel. He had seen it move down the street and had even stepped out to the sidewalk to follow it. He knew that the railroad men were looking for trouble, but there were enough of them so that they could protect themselves against a reasonable onslaught from the saloon men.

There would be bruised knuckles, smashed noses and black eyes, perhaps a broken jaw or head. That was as much damage as men could do with fists. The railroad men were rough, tough fighters. They could hold their own against others. With fists.

Men with guns fought against men with guns. Men with fists fought against men with fists. That was the unwritten law among men. It was the flaw in

Rosser's thinking. He did not anticipate that men with guns would shoot down men without guns.

And so five men were dead.

The survivors of the slaughter came spilling out of the Pleasure Palace and tore down the street, yelling and screaming. Traffic stopped. Men came out of the stores, saloons, but the survivors were too incoherent to give a straight account of what had happened in Condor's saloon. Those on the street, who heard the garbled accounts, could not grasp the enormity of the deed.

Not for moments, that stretched into minutes. And then it was too late.

The marshal and his deputy had reached the Pleasure Palace, were even now coming down the street. Akins carried the wounded man draped over his left shoulder. Ahead of him strode the most calloused man the territory had ever known.

Johnny Honsinger, the official law of Great Plains.

Men saw him, some even who had been present at the slaughter. They gave way before Honsinger as he crossed the street in the van of his burdened deputy.

Sheriff Wes Parker stood in front of the jail. He had been talking to an excited resident of Great Plains, but the attention of both men had been caught by the approach of the marshal and his deputy.

Honsinger said, as he came up, "Riley wants you."

He continued on, to the door of the jail, where he stopped and, turning, coolly surveyed his dominion, the street of Great Plains. Akins, the Deputy, passed him and went into the jail, where he tossed the wounded man on the floor of the marshal's office. There was no room inside the packed cell, which already contained close to a score of prisoners, a number of them still stupefied from whiskey.

Back on the wooden sidewalk, the sheriff looked down the street. Then his eyes went to the hotel. He saw Rosser, headed across to him.

Rosser watched him approach. "Honsinger say how many?" he asked.

The sheriff shook his head. "Enough, if half is true."

"This is the town," Rosser said. "Honsinger's territory."

"I'm still the sheriff," Parker said bleakly. He started to look over his shoulder because he knew that Honsinger was across the street watching, but he caught himself.

"I'd better look into it."

"I'll go with you," Rosser volunteered.

Parker gave him a sharp look, then nodded.

The two men walked silently down the street. As they neared the Pleasure Palace, Parker asked quietly, "You working for the railroad, Tom?"

Rosser gave him a quick look, but made no reply. Without breaking their strides, they turned into the Pleasure Palace, Parker in the lead.

Condor had used the few minutes

since the massacre. The saloon had been vacated of patrons and the help, the bartenders, as well as the gamblers, had moved the bodies of the five dead men out to the alley, behind the saloon. A swamper was already sloshing water over the floor in front of the bar.

At the far end of the bar, a bartender was helping the man with the broken face, trying to stem the flow of blood. That was the scene when the sheriff and Rosser entered the saloon.

Riley Condor, talking to a couple of his gamblers, turned.

"Sheriff," he said. Then he scowled at Rosser. "I've no time for you, Rosser . . ."

"Take time," snapped Rosser.

"Sheriff," Condor said angrily, "you pick some strange friends."

The sheriff made a gesture of dismissal. "I've got to make a report."

"County's your business," said Condor. "Town belongs to the marshal."

"I thought it belonged to you,

Condor," retorted Rosser.

"I'm going to let that pass," Condor said. "There's been enough trouble for one day."

"How many did you kill?" challenged Rosser. "Six . . . a dozen? Some of the people on the street put it as high as twenty . . . "

Condor was white-faced. "Mob comes in here, we have a right to defend ourselves."

"A mob without a gun among them," taunted Rosser.

"Get out of here!" shouted Condor. "Parker, get him out before — "

Parker gripped Rosser's arm. He said, to Condor, "I've still got to make a report . . . "

"Five," snarled Condor. "They're out back in the alley. Now get the hell out — both of you."

"Five," continued Rosser. "A nice, even figure."

Condor whirled and walked into his office, slamming the door behind him.

"Let's go," said Parker to Rosser in a low tone.

Rosser looked deliberately about the big, almost empty saloon. His eyes rested for a moment on Guy Tavenner. The faro dealer sat alone at a table, a whiskey glass clenched in his fist. His eyes evaded Rosser's, but Rosser called to him, "Like this, Tavenner?"

Tavenner refused to look at Rosser.

Parker started for the door, but reaching it, stopped to wait for Rosser. Rosser continued the circuit of the room, with his eyes, his lips parted in a taunting challenge. None in the room kept their eyes on him for more than an instant.

He finally turned and went to the door.

28

JAMES FENIMORE FELL was one of the last persons in Great Plains to hear of the Pleasure Palace massacre. He had worked from early morning steadily through the noon hour, not taking time out to eat.

Time was the element in this huge effort of 1886. They were laying track west from Wolf City, but only so much track could be laid in a single day, so Fell had decided to leapfrog the westward operation, send men and equipment to Great Plains and from there work eastward. The junction would take place somewhere between Wolf City and Great Plains.

That was the reason for the influx of workers into Great Plains. Freighters could haul materials, even rails, to Great Plains. The graders, tracklayers, the hundred or more men who had arrived the day before, were for the eastward operation. They were experienced men, selected from the westward crews.

The trip had been an arduous one, the men had pay coming to them and Fell had given it to them in Great Plains. He had also given them a day's rest, believing that they could attack their work with greater zest.

It was a mistake. Fell did not learn how great a mistake until an hour after the tragedy at Condor's saloon. He had been vaguely aware of the line of shuffling men who were receiving their pay in the other room, but all day he had pored over charts, had talked to foremen and supervisors, freighters and supply men. They had come in and out of his office until he scarcely knew one from another.

Then Bill Daves knocked on his door and entered.

"Yes, Daves," he said impatiently as the superintendent of the Great Plains operation stood before him.

"I think you should know what has happened, Mr. Fell," Daves said soberly. "The men who received their pay today — "

Fell made an impatient gesture. "They got drunk. That's to be expected. Railroad men drink and they fight . . ."

"Yes, sir," conceded Daves, "but . . . five of them have been killed."

Fell's pencil dropped from his hand as he jerked erect.

"What?"

"They were fleeced, swindled of their pay," Daves went on. "They resented it and" — he swallowed hard — "five were murdered, including Sean Kevin."

"Kevin!" exclaimed Fell. "He was in my first crew when we built into Fargo . . ." He pushed back his chair. "How did it happen?"

Daves told him the story as nearly as he was able, from the garbled accounts he had himself received. The single fact of the massacre of five, unarmed men was all that was essential.

Daves was still talking when Fell

came around from the rough desk, passed him and went out. He was not even aware of Susan Tavenner in the other room.

Fell left the railroad building and walked swiftly up the street to the hotel. He strode into the lobby, saw the clerk behind the desk and snapped, "Where's the man who owns this hotel — the Mayor?"

"I — I don't know, sir. He went to a — a meeting, I think . . . "

"Where does the City Council hold its meetings?"

"I couldn't say, Mr. Fell . . . "

"The City Hall — where is it?"

"There isn't any . . . "

Angrily, Fell turned away. At that moment, Rosser came down the stairs. Fell went to him.

"Is it true?"

Rosser nodded. "Five men . . . "

"And where were *you* when it happened?"

"In front of the hotel," Rosser replied evenly. "I saw the mob forming across the street . . . "

"Mob?"

"Some of the railroad men. There seemed to be enough to hold their own." Rosser paused. "I hadn't counted on Condor using guns on unarmed men . . . "

"Condor," Fell said bitterly. "*He* did the shooting?"

"Condor and two of his gunslingers."

"Condor *himself*?" repeated Fell.

"It was in his saloon and Condor *himself* shot down the leader of the mob, a man named Kevin . . . "

"There were witnesses?"

"Enough."

Fell said, "Condor's been arrested?"

Rosser cocked his head to one side. "Who'd arrest him?"

"The man who arrested you. The marshal."

"Mr. Fell," Rosser said patiently, "the marshal is Condor's man. So is the judge."

"Isn't there a sheriff here?"

"There is, but the county, outside of

Great Plains, is his jurisdiction. The town is Honsinger's."

"It's also yours," Fell said emphatically.

Rosser nodded grimly. "With a slight difference. I haven't got the law on my side. I can fight only in self-defense. I tried to make Condor fight last night. I tried again this afternoon."

"Kill him!" snarled Fell. "I don't care how you do it, with the law or without it, but — "

"Mr. Fell," Rosser said patiently, "it isn't just Condor. True, he's the head of the syndicate, but if I kill Condor, Ken Rud takes over and after him, Harold Price . . . and the other saloonkeepers. They're in this for a last-ditch cleanup. You told me that yourself in St. Paul. You also told me that I had to handle the job *without* the aid of the law . . . " He nodded toward the desk. "Where do you think Josh Moody is right now?"

"The clerk said he was attending a council meeting."

"Council meeting? The council consists of Condor and his crowd." Rosser paused. "Moody's attending a meeting of the vigilantes."

"Vigilantes!" gasped Fell.

"I told you they were forming — "

"Get to their meeting," snarled Fell. "Get to their meeting right this minute. Stop them. That's the one thing we can't have here. Word of their formation gets East . . . " Fell gripped Rosser's arm. "Stop them at all costs."

"Mr. Fell," said Rosser, "I doubt if you could stop the vigilantes at this stage."

"I mean it," Fell said fiercely. "Stop them, or so help me . . . "

Rosser pulled his arm free of the railroad magnate's grip, walked past him and went out the dor.

He crossed the street to the unfinished saloon where he had been on trial for his life only the day before. A man wearing a revolver at his belt was leaning against the front door. As

Rosser came up, he straightened.

"Sorry, Mr. Rosser," he said, "you can't go in."

"I've been asked to join," Rosser snapped.

The man regarded him suspiciously. "Who asked you?"

"Doc Kent. Josh Moody."

"I got orders to let no one in."

"Stand aside."

The man glowered at Rosser, but stepped to the right. Rosser pushed past him, opened the door.

In the room, seated on benches left over from the day before, were more than twenty men. Most of them were faces that Rosser had seen around town, merchants.

Dr. Kent sat at the 'judge's' bench. He was the first to see Rosser and said loudly, "Rosser!"

Every head in the room turned.

Dr. Kent said, as Rosser approached, "You're finally throwing in with us?"

"No," said Rosser, "I'm here to stop you."

"Don't try that," Dr. Kent snapped.

Behind Rosser, Josh Moody sprang to his feet.

"Get out of here!" he cried.

Rosser turned and faced the vigilantes. "I know as well as everyone here what happened this afternoon, what's been going on all day. You've only yourselves to blame. You let Condor's crowd rig an election on you. You weren't interested enough at the time . . . "

"Hold on," cried Charlie Hodder. "That's pretty rough language."

"It is. But you're the so-called respectable people of this town. You're the ones that'll be running it when all of this is over and forgotten. That is, you'll be running it if you don't get down to their level. Your kind of people can't fight fire with fire."

"They did it in Virginia City," said Dr. Kent.

"That was twenty-two years ago," retorted Rosser.

"It didn't hurt Colonel Sanders," Josh Moody yelled. "He headed the

Virginia City Vigilantes and became the first United States Senator from Montana."

"You're the Mayor of Great Plains," Rosser went on, "but you won't even be that if you go ahead with your plan."

Wendell Lewis got to his feet. "Mr. Rosser, I'm getting tired of listening to you. I heard you last night and I heard you a couple of nights ago. I don't know what your game is . . . ."

"I have no game!"

"You're a gunfighter, Rosser. Why'd you come to this town?"

"That has nothing to do with this."

"Perhaps it has," said Dr. Kent. "You came here to kill Riley Condor, didn't you?"

"I've made no secret of that," said Rosser grimly. "I'm going to kill him — but I'm going to kill him legally."

"There's no law in this town," Kent snapped. "You found that out yesterday."

"That's the point I'm trying to

make," said Rosser. "You people are the respectable ones of this community. It's up to *you* to make the laws, elect the proper public officials. All right, you got rooked into a rigged election. But you can undo that. Start a recall movement . . . have a new election . . . "

"That takes time. Days, weeks," snapped Josh Moody. "We haven't got the time."

"The five men who were killed this afternoon," Rosser said, "they took the law into their own hands."

Dr. Kent banged his fist on the planks before him. "Gentlemen," he said loudly, "Mr. Rosser's a very eloquent man when he wants to be, but he's also a very inconsistent man. We asked him to join this group. He refused. I now ask for a voice vote. Do you want him to remain — or do you want him to leave?"

An almost unanimous roar of "leave" went up.

"Rosser," the doctor announced, "you heard the opinion. We want you to leave" — his mouth twisted sardonically — "unless you want to try your gun on us . . . "

Rosser turned abruptly and with the eyes of every man in the room on him, walked out of the unfinished saloon.

29

AT five o'clock, Bill Daves said to Susan Tavenner, "Mr. Fell say how long your hours were to be?"

"No," replied Susan.

"You were here this morning at seven, weren't you?"

"Yes. I understand that is when the men — "

"The men work ten hours, with an hour for dinner at noon. But since you're a woman — "

"I'll work the same as a man," Susan said quickly.

"From seven until six?"

"Yes."

Daves shrugged. "I guess that's up to you — or Mr. Fell."

"Me," said Susan.

Daves grinned. "Gonna take me a while to get used to a woman working here."

As yet, Susan was not aware of what had happened in the town that day. She had heard shooting, but she had heard shooting before. She knew that the railroad men had been paid, because she had assisted in that job and she knew also — vaguely — that men with money in their pockets drank whiskey. And gambled. She knew more about the latter than about the drinking.

She had heard men come in and talk excitedly, but the work that had been given her, checking bills of lading against receipts and tallies, had occupied her mind, since the last man had been paid that morning.

She got her first inkling of what had happened in the town when she left the railroad office a few minutes after six and walked to the hotel.

In the hotel lobby, James Fell sat on a chair just inside the door. "Mrs. Tavenner," he said when she entered, "I'd advise you not to leave the hotel this evening."

She was surprised. "Why?"

"Because of what's happened. You've heard . . . ?"

She shook her head.

"There's been trouble. Some of our men, they — they've been hurt."

"By Mr. Rosser?"

Fell looked at her sharply. "Why do you say *Rosser*?"

"I — I don't know. Only . . . " She bit her lower lip with her sharp white teeth. "His reputation," she added lamely.

"You know about that!"

"I guess everyone does."

"Yet you're friendly with him . . . !"

"Friendly?"

Fell said, "You're a married woman, but Rosser asked me to put you to work."

"Oh, no," Susan exclaimed in dismay.

Fell held up a hand. "I was considering the matter anyway, but I hadn't made up my mind when he spoke on your behalf."

Susan took refuge in the previous

subject. "What — what happened today?"

"Five of our men were killed. Not by Rosser. By the murderers who seem to have control of this town." Fell added heavily, "As a matter of fact, I had hoped that *Mister* Rosser would be able to prevent such things."

"But how can he? He — he isn't the marshal."

"You're now an employee of the railroad. You'll be seeing Mr. Rosser coming and going. I don't want it spread around, but he is working for the railroad." He stopped. Josh Moody had entered the hotel.

"Mr. Moody!" Fell called sharply.

The Mayor of Great Plains winced when he saw the railroad man. He came toward him.

Fell nodded to Susan. "Later, Mrs. Tavenner . . ."

Susan headed for the stairs, as the mayor stopped before Fell.

"I'm sorry about what happened . . ." Moody began.

"*You're* sorry!" snapped Fell. "Those men worked for me."

"I know, sir. Something is going to be done about it."

"Who's going to do it? Your vigilantes, Moody?"

"Vigilantes, Mr. Fell, have been necessary before. In San Francisco, in eighteen fifty-four . . . "

"And Virginia City in 'sixty-four!" snapped Fell. "But there'll be none in Great Plains."

"Mr. Fell," Moody said earnestly, "you are not a resident of Great Plains. *I* am."

"This is my town!"

"Is it, Mr. Fell? I was under the impression that the people who live here — "

"I laid out this town. I sold you your business lots."

"That is true," Moody admitted. "Nevertheless, when you sold us the property, you gave us the right to make our own laws, run the city as we . . . " Moody hesitated, realizing that he had gotten on dangerous ground.

"Go on," Fell prodded. "I gave you the right to elect your own officials. You chose a bunch of thieves, murderers!"

"Yes," said Moody hoarsely, "but we intend to rectify that."

"With vigilantes?"

"With vigilantes, if necessary. And it *has* become necessary."

"No!" thundered Fell.

"Mr. Fell," protested Moody, "you know what happened today. They were your own employees . . ."

"They were," shouted Fell, "and I'm going to make Condor and his crowd pay for that, but it'll be done without vigilantes. Understand?"

"No," said Moody stubbornly. "The people of this community — "

Fell got to his feet. "The hell with the people of this community! They'll ruin me if I don't stop them. You blithering idiot, don't you know that I've sunk every dollar I could beg, borrow, or steal — steal, into this venture? Don't you know I've risked *everything* to build this railroad and that I *must* have an uninterrupted flow of immigrants to make it pay? Word of vigilantes gets on the telegraph wire, it'll stop immigration like *that*! And people *must* come here. I need their money."

Moody said bleakly, "What's the use of their coming here if they're going to be murdered when they arrive?"

"There'll be no more murdering," snapped Fell.

Moody said angrily, "*You're* going to make a law against it?"

Fell said dangerously, "I'm warning you — I want no vigilantes!"

30

ANOTHER meeting was going on in Great Plains, even as the vigilantes met in the unfinished saloon across from the hotel.

Riley Condor had tremendous powers of mental recuperation. Minutes after the slaughter in his saloon, he was anticipating possible retaliation. Messengers went out, and shortly afterward Parker and Rosser left the Pleasure Palace.

Condor kept the back door of his office unlocked, for he knew that certain of the people he had sent for would prefer to enter by the alley door.

They began to come. Rud, Price, Fred Wagoner. Within a half hour there was fifteen men, besides Condor, in the saloon. None were employees of Condor's. Those had been dismissed for the time being, with the exception of certain ones who stood guard in the alley, or in front of the Pleasure Palace.

The callers straggled in and the discussions began after the first two or three arrived. Future policies were already being laid down by the time the majority were gathered around a faro layout.

The 'meeting' at the unfinished saloon up the street was already known to most of those present.

"They're forming a Vigilante Committee," Ken Rud snapped. "Been hearin' about it for days, but this is going to make them move."

The word 'vigilante' caused an uneasy exchange of glances among some of the men present but Condor, who was at his best in these moments, banged a fist on the faro table.

"Vigilantes be damned! They're a bunch of yellow-bellied, chicken-hearted ribbon clerks. About four of them have fired rifles before. Two, revolvers."

"But there's a crowd of them,"

growled one of the men.

"How big a crowd? Fifteen? Twenty?"

"All of that," said Rud.

"That many came here an hour ago," snapped Condor. "They started running when the first shot was fired."

He took a sheet of paper from his pocket. "I've made a rough list of the men we control. Counting bartenders, dealers, roustabouts . . . I've got twelve men on my payroll. Rud, how many have *you* got?"

"Ten."

"I had you down for nine. Price?"

"Ten — two more'n I really need."

"You'll need them now." Condor nodded in satisfaction. "I had us down for between sixty and sixty-five men. There seem to be a few more. About two thirds of our people know which end of a gun a bullet comes from. Which is more than I can say about the vigilantes. And one thing they haven't got and we have" — Condor smirked — "Law. *We're the law*."

He picked up a cigar box from the

faro table and upended it. A stream of nickled badges spilled out upon the table.

"I bought these last winter, just in case. Our people are going to be wearing *these*."

There was some discussion about that, but Condor silenced it by banging on the faro table with the muzzle of his revolver.

"We're in this, all of us. The trouble happened to be here this afternoon. It could just as well have been in any one of your places. Every damn one of you is using faro boxes, every one of you has some slick boys dealing poker. We invested our money in this town, and we're going to get it back. That's all there's to it."

Ten minutes later, the men began leaving, one and two at a time, some by the front door, some by the alley. Condor signaled certain men to remain behind: Ken Rud, Harold Price, a man named Tepperman.

"All right, we've got twenty men

deputized," Condor said then. "That's for the showdown with the vigilantes. They'll be ready day and night and they can get to any point around town in from three to five minutes. That's fine. But there's just one thing more . . . Tom Rosser."

"I was wondering when you were going to get around to him," Ken Rud said quietly.

"Let's face it," Condor said, "the man's dangerous. He proved that last night."

"He's in with the vigilantes?" Price asked.

Condor hesitated. "I would say no. He's a lone wolf by nature. He knows what he's doing. He proved that yesterday. He *wants* people to draw on him."

"What about Honsinger?" asked Tepperman.

"Perhaps," said Condor, "perhaps not. I've got an ace in the hole, but I want to hold that until I *have* to show it." He drew a deep breath. "The entire vigilante crowd isn't as dangerous as Tom Rosser."

"What I was going to say," Price offered. "The way he come into my place last night . . . " He shook his head.

"Four years ago," Condor said, "a boy nobody ever heard of put a bullet through Jesse James's head. Why?"

"Reward money."

Condor nodded. "Whisper it to some of your best boys. Tell them there's a thousand dollars for the man who gets Rosser. Fair or foul, it makes no difference. Gold."

"I'll give five hundred myself," growled Rud.

"You, Price?"

"I'll go five hundred."

"I'll go along for five," said Tepperman.

"All right, pass the word along. Twenty-five hundred. Cash on the barrel. *And* a fast horse, if the man wants it."

An hour later, twenty men wearing

badges knew of the two-thousand-five hundred dollars bounty for the head of Tom Rosser. Each of the twenty, inside of a couple more hours, told at least one other man. By nine o'clock that evening, half the people in Great Plains knew of it.

During the temporary lockout of the employees of the Pleasure Palace, Guy Tavenner was at loose ends. He had moved from the hotel the day before to one of the rooms on the upper floor of the Pleasure Palace, but that was forbidden to him during the secret meeting of Condor and his syndicate.

And Tavenner was not keen on walking down the street of Great Plains. He had shot a man in the arm that day and his face was familiar to a good many of the railroadmen.

It was five o'clock when he was driven from the Pleasure Palace. He walked down the alley to the rear of the hotel and stood for awhile studying the hotel.

He scowled at the two-story frame

building, then walked to the door through which supplies were taken into the hotel. He tried the door. It was locked from the inside.

Tavenner took a knife from his pocket and slipped the blade in the door crack. Inside of ten seconds he had slipped the bolt inside.

He entered the hotel. Straight ahead was a hallway that ran to the kitchen. To Tavenner's right was a staircase leading to the second floor. He climbed the stairs, reached the second-floor landing.

His former room was just ahead, but he had turned in his key the day before. The room was probably rented again. But his wife still had her room.

He moved toward it, listened a moment.

There was no sound inside. He tried the doorknob furtively. The door was locked, but the slight grating sound would have been heard in the room. There was still no sound, so Tavenner guessed that his wife, as he called her in his thoughts, was not in her room. Probably down in the lobby waiting for Rosser, hoping to catch sight of him.

Thoughts of Rosser suddenly angered Tavenner. He had shot a man that morning. It was easy enough; all one had to do was draw quick — get the drop on the opponent, and shoot.

Rosser was not invulnerable.

So thinking, Tavenner again drew out his pocket-knife and inside of thirty seconds was opening the door.

The room was in semidarkness because the shade had been drawn — and it was empty.

Tavenner closed the door and sniffed. She still had some of her perfume. He could smell it. He crossed the room, raised the shade a foot so that there was sufficient light in the room. Then, methodically, he searched the place.

There were very few of her possessions here, most of them having been left in the St. Paul hotel, but what there was he searched. He found nothing — which annoyed him.

He had *hoped* to find something. What he did not know exactly. Something incriminating that would link her — to Rosser?

Tavenner glowered at the eastern wall, beyond which was Rosser's room, although there were two rooms in between his wife's and Rosser's. The day before Rosser had heard her scream. Well, *that* would not happen again.

Tavenner sat down on the bed.

He had come to Great Plains with less than twenty dollars in his pocket. All he had was a statement from Riley Condor — by letter — that he could use a good man. He had gone into the Pleasure Palace, not as a partner, but as an employee.

Ten dollars a day, plus twenty per cent of the winnings. His game had won eight hundred dollars today. One hundred and sixty dollars of it would come to Tavenner. A comforting sum of money. Plus his wage of the past few days . . . a stake of over two hundred.

It wasn't enough.

Tavenner had no liking for Great Plains, and did not care for the way things were shaping up. He had seen the slaughter in the Pleasure Palace just a short while ago and he knew, as did every man in the territory, that Montana had a record of vigilantes. The word had been tossed around Great Plains. If he had a thousand dollars in his pocket he would buy a horse — or steal one — and shake the dust of Great Plains.

But Riley Condor had not yet paid him and in his pocket was something like seven dollars.

He stretched out on the bed. He had been a gambler for most of his adult life and as a gambler, he had had his ups and downs. Sometimes he had been affluent and had spent his money like water — no, not water like champagne. There had been lean times, too, but never before had he had such a long run of lean times.

He had counted on Great Plains to

recoup his fortunes. The last of the big boom towns, Riley Condor had told him. That was probably true. But how could a man mend his fortunes if he couldn't have a long enough run with the cards.

His bad luck had begun . . . back in Indiana, when he had met and married Susan, his wife. Damn, he had never been forced to marry a woman before, not since the time in New Orleans, what was it . . . nine years ago? These sweet, innocent ones. They *had* to have marriage. And then they gave a man nothing but trouble.

Tavenner's mind was running along those lines, so that he did not hear the footsteps outside the door. It was the key turning in the lock that brought him up.

Then he moved like lightning. He was off the bed, reaching for Susan as she came in through the door.

His hand clapped over her mouth, stifling a scream. He nudged the door shut, shot the bolt with his free hand as she struggled to get free of the grip he held on her mouth. The door closed — and locked — Tavenner had his left hand free and he wrapped it around Susan.

"Not a peep out of you," he snarled into her ear.

31

SUSAN lay on the bed, dry-eyed. Her mouth was bruised from where Tavenner had gripped her; there were bruises on her throat where he had choked her. Two days ago she had told herself that this would never happen to her again. But it had. She had not had the physical strength to fight him off.

And during the humiliation of it she could not cry out.

She lay now, on the bed, in the darkend room.

There was a light knock on the door. Susan made no reply. The knock was repeated.

"Yes," she called.

"Rosser," came the careful voice from outside the door.

"Come in," Susan said listlessly.

The door was opened a few inches.

Rosser stopped as he noted that the room was dark.

"It's all right," Susan said. "Come in."

Rosser swung the door open wider and with only the light from over his shoulder, made out Susan lying on the bed. In his wildest moments of fancy — and he had few such moments — he had never expected to see her thus.

He said, "I'm sorry."

"You're sorry," Susan said. "I'm sorry. Everybody's sorry. Everybody but Guy Tavenner."

"He's been here!" Rosser said abruptly.

She was silent a moment and Rosser began to back out of the room.

Then Susan spoke again: "He was here when I came in. He — he choked me."

"I didn't think he had that much spunk."

"Oh, Guy's a very brave man. Against a woman. Especially his wife, who can't defend herself, even by calling for help . . . " A sudden shudder shook her and the tears finally came. Tears and sobs.

This was beyond Rosser's experience. Carol Grannan had never wept. Nor had she ever invited Rosser to come into her bedroom. Not until that last — no, it had not been she, even then.

The invitation had been sent to Tom Rosser by the man from Idaho . . . the man who had been brought to Broken Lance by Riley Condor, who was now in Great Plains.

And who was still alive.

He backed out of the room, closing the door behind him. He passed his own room and descended the stairs to the hotel lobby.

Josh Moody was not in the lobby, but as Rosser came down the stairs he saw Joe Leach go behind the desk and enter Moody's private room. Rosser caught a glimpse of Charlie Hodder and Dr. Kent already in the room.

The vigilantes were having another meeting.

312

Across the street in the marshal's office, Johnny Honsinger stared at Sim Akins.

"Twenty-five hundred dollars?" he exclaimed. "For that much money I'd — " He stopped. "Who told you?"

"Man in Rud's place. Rud's putting up part of the money, I guess."

"You guess? You don't know for sure?" Anger twisted Honsinger's face. "If Rud's in it, so's Condor and he never said a damn thing about it."

"Why don't you ask him?"

"I'm going to do just that," snapped Honsinger. He hitched up his gunbelt and left the marshal's office. He had been gone less than two minutes when Sheriff Parker entered.

"Where's the marshal?"

"Gone to see Riley Condor."

Parker nodded toward the open cell door. "You let the prisoners go?"

"Too much trouble feeding 'em," retorted Akins. "Judge Murcott fined them each twenty-five dollars. Jim Fell paid for the lot." He frowned. "Three of them was bleedin' all over the place. I guess Doc Kent had himself a time today."

"And you, Akins?" asked Parker. "What kind of time have you had today?"

Akins grimaced. "A little more'n I figured on, when Riley pinned the star on me." He shrugged. "But the pay's good."

"What're you getting?"

Hundred a month — and three dollars for every arrest," he grinned. "I made myself thirty-three dollars today."

"Chicken feed," said Parker easily. "Especially when you can make twenty-five hundred dollars . . ."

"Hey," exclaimed Akins. "You heard about that?"

"I heard it, but I didn't believe it."

"It's all around town. I told Johnny and *he* wouldn't believe it either. He's down at Condor's now checking."

"Anybody got a better chance than Johnny?"

Parker shook his head. "I knew a man once who tried to shoot another man in the back for two thousand . . . "

"He make it?"

"He missed . . . and killed a woman instead."

"That's the way the ball bounces," Atkins said. "He get the two thousand?"

"He got it," said Parker, as he left the marshal's office.

Outside, Parker stood in the darkness. There was light coming from the doors and windows of the saloons, but the traffic on the street was light. There would be little play at the faro and poker tables tonight.

Yet, there were men on the street. They stood in front of the saloons in pairs, and here and there, in a dark doorway, stood other men. Now and then they moved and light from a distant window flashed on metal the men wore. Deputies' badges.

Parker cossed the street to the hotel. There was a shadow on the veranda, and he stopped at the bottom of the short flight of stairs that led up to the veranda.

"Rosser?" he called carefully.

"Yes, Wes," was the reply from the shadow.

Parker moved closer, searched the shadows to make sure that no one else was on the veranda. "Were you planning to go out tonight?"

"And walk into a trap?" Rosser shook his head. "One thing I never said about Riley Condor — that he was stupid."

Parker said carefully, "There's talk that a man can get himself twenty-five hundred dollars by taking care of you."

"*Any* man?"

"Any man with a bullet in his gun."

"Well, that's something new," Rosser said. "Back in Kansas, Condor put a price on me. But he brought in a special man for the job. A man from Idaho . . ."

"There are a lot of new badges around Great Plains," Parker said bleakly. "One more or less won't

316

be noticed." He paused. "I've often wondered what California was like."

"It's sand," said Rosser. "Sand and mountains . . . and people. They're the same as anywhere else. You're not the running-away type, Wes. You'll play out the hand."

"You, Tom?"

"Riley Condor's *here*. He isn't in California, or anywhere else . . . "

"The syndicate's got a lot of guns. You can't watch them all. Sometime you're got to turn your back."

Rosser said evenly, "I know that."

32

THE vigilantes began to gather
at Leach's livery stable at four
o'clock in the morning. It was
the first morning in weeks that the
town was stilled. Always until now
there had been lights in the saloons,
activity. This morning there was none.

It should have warned the vigilantes,
but they were dedicated men. They
assembled in the stable in the semidarkness, since Leach kept only the
single night lantern burning.

All of the men carried rifles or
shotguns. A few had revolvers. Wendell
Lewis, the storekeeper, brought a half
dozen coils of brand-new rope.

There was very little talk. All
the plans had been laid the night
before. They would assemble at four
o'clock and in a body move to the
headquarters of the syndicate, Riley

Condor's Pleasure Palace. There they would apprehend Condor himself, and such of his cohorts as were on a list prepared by the vigilantes the day before: gamblers, dealers who had made themselves conspicuous. Guy Tavenner's name was on the list.

After Condor, the vigilantes would swing back, pick up Harold Price, Ken Rud and others up and down the street. There were twenty-two names on the lists in the hands of the vigilantes. The rest would be exiled, driven from Great Plains — Montana.

At four twenty, with the false dawn faint in the sky, the vigilantes counted heads. There were sixteen men in the group. Twenty-eight had been counted on the night before. Twelve vigilantes had 'overslept.' Lost their nerve.

Dr. Kent said, "We've enough men for the job." The doctor carried a double-barreled English shotgun, as well as a Frontier Model, thrust behind the waistband of his striped trousers.

The vigilantes moved out into the

street. Beyond the jail, a man stepped out of the shadows, raised his hand into the air. A revolver fired twice quickly, then twice more, at longer intervals.

Josh Moody exclaimed, "That's a signal!"

Shadows moved ahead on both sides of the street. Men darted out of doorways, ran between buildings, or whipped across the street for chosen vantage points.

The vigilantes, nevertheless, continued down the street. Lights were on in the Pleasure Palace, but as the vigilantes came close, the lights winked out one by one.

A voice called from the darkness, "That's far enough!"

Dr. Kent said loudly, "Condor? You're under arrest . . . "

Another man — Johnny Honsinger — laughed raucously. "You're arresting who? You're a mob. *We're* the law."

"We'll give you a trial, Condor," Dr. Kent continued. "That's more than you gave those men yesterday."

"I'll count three," replied the voice of Honsinger. "If you ain't runnin' by then, we start shooting . . . One . . . "

Dr. Kent fired at the dark front of the Pleasure Palace. Honsinger did not have to count up to two. The doctor's shot was signal enough.

Flame lanced the darkness from a dozen different directions. Guns cracked in front, to the right, to the left, in the rear. The vigilantes were completely enfiladed and only the almost total darkness saved them from utter and quick extinction.

The fight lasted less than thirty seconds, although a few scattered shots continued beyond that time. The vigilantes were routed completely. Some of them fired once or twice, but whether they scored even a single hit was dubious.

The vigilantes were not so fortunate. They had been in a clump, had revealed their position by the challenges of Dr. Kent, the leader of the vigilantes.

Three vigilantes remained where they

fell. Others limped, dragged or crawled out of the way.

The signal shots awakened Rosser. Save for his boots and coat, he had not been undressing lately. He swung his feet to the floor and sat still listening.

He did not hear the voices that preceded the opening of the battle, but he knew what was coming.

He had not long to wait. During the thirty seconds of gunfire, he pulled on his boots and buckled his cartridge belt about him. The shooting had stopped as he left his room and descended to the hotel lobby.

Ordinarily, there would have been a light in the lobby, but Josh Moody had taken certain precautions before leaving to join his friends at the livery stable and the lobby was in complete darkness.

Rosser called out as he came down to the lobby.

"Clerk?"

"Wh-who is it?" came a frightened voice from the region of the desk.

"Rosser!"

He moved forward, crossing to the door. Boots pounded the sidewalk outside and then the door was flung open. A man rushed into the hotel.

"Don't strike a light!" he cried. "It's me — Moody."

Rosser said, "You got licked, Moody. I tried to warn you . . . "

Moody whirled. "You, Rosser," he cried bitterly. "You wouldn't join us, but you're here now to gloat."

"I'm not going to rub it in, Moody," Rosser replied. "I came down just in case . . . " He paused. "How bad was it?"

"Terrible!" groaned Moody. "I — I don't know if more than two or three of us got away." He began to curse savagely. "Half never showed up. The chicken-hearted bastards. They talked big, but when it came to the showdown, they didn't have the guts . . . "

"Mobs are usually that way."

"Mobs?" cried Moody.

"Vigilantes are mobs," Rosser said

firmly. Then he became aware of a sudden groan in the darkness. "You're hit Moody!"

"My — my head," moaned the Mayor of Great Plains. "I thought it was just a scratch, but . . ." A cry of anguish was torn from him, then Rosser heard the thud of his body as Moody dropped to the floor.

"Put on a light," he snapped, moving forward.

His foot touched the soft body of Moody and he dropped to his knees. His hands went along the body, to Moody's face. He felt warm stickiness.

"I said a light!" he snarled.

A match was struck behind the desk. It failed to ignite, and it was a full second before the match was again struck. By the feeble light, Rosser picked up Moody and by the time he got to the rear of the desk, the wall lamp was lit.

He pushed open the door of Moody's private room. The clerk followed him. "Shut the door," Rosser said angrily.

"And put on a light in here."

The match, this time, was ignited with the first scratch. Rosser saw the cot across the room and carried Moody to it.

The mayor was moaning softly.

Rosser got the lamp from the table, brought it to the cot. He thrust it into the hand of the clerk. "Hold it close." He bent over Moody and already knowing where to look, examined the wound on the side of Moody's head.

It was no more than a deep cut. Shock had carried Moody to the hotel, the reaction had set in and he had collapsed. The slight wound would scarcely require the services of Dr. Kent . . . if Dr. Kent was still able to care for patients.

Rosser got water, found some sheets in a closet and ripped off strips. He had washed the wound and was about to bandage it when the door of the room was pushed in by Dr. Kent.

"You, Rosser," the doctor growled.

Dr. Kent came across the room, bent

over Josh Moody. "It's just a crease." He took the bandage from Rosser, began twisting it about the Mayor's head. Moody groaned and tried to sit up.

"In a minute, Josh," the doctor said.

He tucked in the end of the bandage, gave the mayor a hand to help him to a sitting position. Moody shook his head, winced and looked at Kent, then at Rosser.

"How bad was it?" he asked.

"Plenty bad," the doctor replied.

Rosser noted then the soggy, dark stain on the doctor's own left arm. "You stopped one yourself, Doctor," he said.

Kent shook his head. "A flesh wound." He regarded Rosser thoughtfully. "We walked into the trap."

Rosser shrugged. "What did you expect?"

"Nothing — from you!" snapped Josh Moody. "You'll do me a favor by getting your luggage and moving to hell out of this hotel."

"You may have your room soon enough," Rosser said.

"By noon?"

"In a day or two."

"You'll get out today."

"Josh," said Dr. Kent, "you can't blame Rosser for our failure."

"If he isn't with us, he's against us."

"That's why Condor's put a price of twenty-five hundred on my scalp?" Rosser asked drily.

Moody stared at him. "That's nonsense!"

"I heard about it." Kent looked sharply at Rosser. "It isn't just a rumor?"

Rosser shrugged. "Maybe that's all it is — a rumor."

He walked out.

In the lobby, fully dressed, was James Fenimore Fell. He was pacing savagely back and forth. As Rosser came around the desk, Fell saw him.

"Here you are! I banged on your door . . . " He strode toward Rosser, brandishing his fist.

"I told you to stop the vigilantes," he raged. "I warned you what would happen if you didn't."

"What's going to happen?"

"You're through. Fired!"

"All right," said Rosser. "I'm fired. Now fire the vigilantes . . ."

"They'll listen to me, or I'll break them, every mother's son of them. I'll ruin them. That's what they've done to me and so help me . . ."

Rosser pointed to the door behind the desk. "The two leading vigilantes are in there. Go ahead — tell them what you're going to do to them . . ."

"You think I won't?"

Fell gave Rosser a contemptuous look and strode behind the desk. He slammed opened the door and stormed into the hotelman-mayor's room. For a moment, Rosser heard the rumbling of Fell's voice as he denounced the vigilantes. Then the sharper voice of Dr. Kent interrupted and was shouted down by the roar of Jim Fell's most thundering denunciation.

328

33

THE real dawn was lightening the sky as Rosser left the hotel and stood on the veranda.

The syndicate's guards were again posted at strategic points around the street. In front of Riley Condor's Pleasure Palace were several shapeless forms. Vigilantes, who had been left where they had fallen.

As Rosser watched, the sheriff stepped out of the marshal's office across the street. Rosser crossed to him, but as he stepped up on the porch, Johnny Honsinger came out of the office.

"You with those so-called Vigilantes?" he asked nastily.

"If it meant anything," Rosser said deliberately, "I wouldn't give you the time of day, but since you're through, I don't mind telling you. No, I wasn't with them."

"Through?" snarled Honsinger. "Who say's I'm through?"

"You licked some of the people," Rosser said, "but you can't lick *all* of the people and inside of a day or two, three days at the most, you're going to have to face *all* of the people in this town. And then you're through." He looked at the sheriff. "Tell him, Sheriff."

"Nobody can tell him anything," Parker said soberly.

"I'm getting fed up with you," the marshal snarled at Parker. "You ain't doin' a damn bit of good here to anybody. You might just as well climb on your horse and get back to wherever the hell you came from."

"I may do that, Johnny," the sheriff said, "after I've attended your funeral."

"You want to try for that funeral?" Honsinger asked ominously. "Just say the word . . . "

"Perhaps I will," said the sheriff. "When I'm ready."

He turned his back on the marshal

and re-entered the office. Honsinger shifted his glowering eyes on Rosser. "That goes for you, old man. Any time — any place!"

Rosser did not bother to reply to the kill-crazy young marshal. He recrossed the street to the hotel and took up his usual vigil, three feet to the right of the door.

From here he could see up the street and down the street. And across.

Fell came storming out of the hotel some minutes later. He saw Rosser and stopped for one last shout at him. "I meant that, Rosser. You're through."

Rosser made no reply and Fell clumped down the steps. He turned to the right and went toward the railroad buildings. It was a few minutes after five.

Twenty minutes later, Dr. Kent came out of the hotel. He said to Rosser. "You could have told us . . . that you were working for the railroad."

"I'm not working for them now."

The doctor nodded. "Fell said he's

fired you. Nothing to keep you from joining us now."

Rosser shook his head. "With the railroad's backing, or without it, I'm against vigilantes."

"What the hell are you *for*?" the doctor snapped.

"I told you," Rosser repeated. "I came to Great Plains for one reason only — to kill Riley Condor."

Dr. Kent stared at him, then shaking his head, he turned and went across the street to his office where he had patients already waiting for him. Vigilantes who had made it that far.

The sun came up in the heavens and the town of Great Plains slowly came to life. Men ventured upon the street. At six o'clock Riley Condor himself appeared, saw the bodies of the vigilantes lying out in the street and called some of his henchmen. They removed the bodies, taking them into the alley from where they would eventually be taken to 'boot hill,' the thriving new cemetery a half mile from town.

A couple of merchants opened their stores.

Men passed Rosser, went into the hotel. Some of them had fresh bandages on their heads, their arms. Guests came apprehensively out of the hotel, surveyed the quiet street, then either went back inside or darted off to various destinations. Some of them went to Mary Donley's restaurant.

At ten minutes to seven Susan Tavenner came out of the hotel. She caught a sideward glimpse of Rosser standing beside the door, winced and hurried down the stairs. Then she stopped and came back.

"Mr. Rosser," she said, her face a fiery crimson, "how — how can I get a gun?"

"Most any stores. The hardware . . ." He nodded toward Wendell Lewis's store. "Lewis carries a full line, unless he's given them all to the vigilantes."

"Vigilantes?"

"Haven't you heard about what happened this morning? Early . . . "

She shuddered. "Yes, the — the waitress told me at breakfast. And Mr. Moody's been hurt."

"A gun may be a handy thing to carry around," said Rosser. "Even for a woman."

Her eyes dropped, then came up again to meet his. She said, "I think you know why I want a gun."

He was on the verge of asking her, 'Why?' but saw that she was determined to give him the answer, and actually preferred that she not be led into it.

He waited, and she said, "I want the gun for . . . "

And then she faltered and could not bring it out.

He said, "Your husband."

"For Guy Tavenner," she burst out, then fled.

Rosser was still looking after her when Josh Moody came out upon the veranda.

"I shall expect your room by noon," he said stiffly.

"You're going to press it?" Rosser asked.

"I am," Moody said stubbornly.

Rosser nodded.

34

IT was eight o'clock in the morning and Guy Tavenner sat at his faro table, a glass of whiskey in his fist, a half-emptied bottle at his elbow.

He had been sitting there since the repulse of the vigilantes, shortly after four o'clock. He had not slept, having been alerted along with the other dealers and hangers-on of the Pleasure Palace. He had emptied his gun in the general direction of the ill-fated vigilante party, and he may even have hit a vigilante or two.

But he was not thinking of the vigilantes.

He was thinking of his wife and, mostly, he was thinking of himself.

He had been in other boom towns in the West. He had dealt faro in Dodge City, in Cheyenne and he had even taught the game to the

Canadians during the building of their own transcontinental railroad.

It was not the same. Always before there had been a semblance of law and order. You carried a gun, but it wasn't often that you had to use it. There was always The Law in the crucial spots.

In Great Plains there was no law. There were men with badges, but they were hirelings of the lawless element. Tavenner's own class, for that matter.

Life, Tavenner told his whiskey-blurred brain, was too cheap in Great Plains. It was no place for a man like Guy Tavenner, who in recent years had dealt cards to the elite of Chicago, St. Louis, New Orleans. Men did not raise their voices in those places. They did not smash dealers in the face, or draw guns on them.

There had been no vigilantes in the gambling saloons of Chicago and St. Louis, New Orleans.

There had been no professional gunfighters such as Tom Rosser.

Rosser.

Every time his thickened tongue mumbled the name, Tavenner took another drink of whiskey. Since midnight he had drunk a quart of the stuff. A quart and a half. Enough to put another man under the table in blessed unconsciousness, where he could no longer think. But Tavenner was an experienced toper. He drank slowly, relishing the fiery stuff, swishing it around in his mouth. He had been drinking for four hours.

Rosser.

Susan.

She had made a fool of him in St. Paul. When butter wouldn't melt in her mouth, when she had protested at his gambling, his drinking, she had been seeing Rosser even then. Had been . . .

His hand hurled the shot glass away from him. He groped for another glass, could not find one. He gripped the bottle, tilted it to his mouth and spilled about two glassfuls for the swallow of whiskey he actually got into his mouth.

It was then that Riley Condor came out of his private office and saw Tavenner with the bottle to his mouth. He came up.

"You drunken fool," Condor said. "What the devil do you think you're doing?"

Tavenner lowered the bottle and focused his eyes on the man before him. He knew it was Condor, but he had difficulty in recognizing him.

"Condor," he said thickly, "I want my pay. I'm getting out of this town and I want my pay . . . "

"You've been drinking it up, you sot," sneered Condor. He gestured to a bartender. "You charging this man for his whiskey?"

"Yes, Mr. Condor," was the reply. "That's his second bottle."

"It's also his last," snapped Condor. He reached for the half-filled bottle in Tavenner's fist. "Give me that . . . "

Tavenner was too drunk. Sober, even half sober, he was deathly afraid of Riley Condor. In his present condition he was not afraid of . . . anyone.

He said drunkenly, "Gimme my pay, or by goddam . . . " he started to swing the whiskey bottle at the hazy figure before him, missed by inches, but cracked the bottle against the edge of the table.

Riley Condor came around the table in three swift strides. He reached out with his left hand, caught the lapels of Tavenner's Prince Albert and half-raising him from the chair, whipped his right hand across Tavenner's face and back.

Tavenner gasped and the stink of his breath angered Riley Condor even more. He yanked Tavenner to his feet, caught him by the scruff of his neck with one hand and by the seat of his trousers with the other, and rushed him toward the batwing doors. In his younger years, Riley Condor has been a bouncer in a trail-town saloon and he had not lost the knack of giving a man the 'bum's rush.'

He propelled Tavenner headlong at

the batwing doors, gave a final heave and let go.

Tavenner came through the swinging doors, landed on his face on the wooden sidewalk and for a moment lay completely motionless. Then his stomach retched and he heaved up about a pint of the alcohol he had imbibed.

Fell had gone to his work without breakfast. At seven thirty he began to become even more irritable than he had been, and decided that he might as well have something to eat.

He returned to the hotel and ate a substantial breakfast. He came out of the hotel at the exact moment that Guy Tavenner was given the heave-ho by Riley Condor a hundred yards up the street.

It was also the exact moment that Susan Tavenner came out of Wendell Lewis's store across the street. She had gone to work at seven o'clock, directly after her scene with Tom Rosser before the hotel. She had gone to the railroad offices with an obsession — the need to buy a gun. She could not get it out of her mind and when Fell had left the offices to get his breakfast, Susan stopped her work and stared at the desk before her.

She *had* to have the gun. Possession of it would give her relief. Guy Tavenner would not again come into her room and do to her what he had done the night before.

She got up suddenly from her desk and said to Bill Daves, who was working across the room, "I've got to do an errand!"

On these three isolated incidents hung the fate of Great Plains.

Guy Tavenner, drunk, had the courage to swing a whiskey bottle at Riley Condor.

James Fenimore Fell, railroad building, ate a belated breakfast.

Susan Tavenner felt a compulsion to buy a gun.

Fell came out of the hotel, saw Rosser standing beside the door. Angrily he stamped down to the sidewalk and saw Susan Tavenner leaving the general store of Wendell Lewis.

He called to her across the street, "Mrs. Tavenner!"

He called loudly and Guy Tavenner, reeling away from the Pleasure Palace, heard the name Tavenner. His bleary eyes looked toward the hotel, saw a man waving.

He broke into a rubber-legged run.

Susan heard her employer, located him and started across the street toward him. Fell, knowing he would have to cross the street and having called to his employee only to walk back to the office with her, started across the street.

Tavenner came toward them, saw a man and a woman he identified vaguely as his wife crossing the street toward each other to meet in the center of the street.

"You filthy . . . " mouthed Tavenner

as he came running toward the two people in the street.

It was then that Susan Tavenner saw her husband. Her hand went instinctively into her bag, which contained the article she had just purchased in Wendell Lewis's store. There was only one thing wrong. She had purchased a box of cartridges but had not loaded the revolver. In fact, did not know *how* to load it. She had intended to practice that evening.

So, her hand gripped the revolver in her purse, but did not draw it.

Tavenner was now leaving the sidewalk, weaving drunkenly as he approached Fell and Susan.

Then a dozen feet from the two he stopped abruptly. The man before him was not Tom Rosser. It was . . . the Big Man. The railroad builder. *He* was having a tryst with Tavenner's wife.

"You," he mouthed, "you, too!" He tried to point a wavering finger at Susan. "You've been sleeping with *him*. You . . ."

He said a word.

Fell strode toward the drunken man and slapped his face hard.

Tavenner had been struck only minutes before by Riley Condor. There had been no humiliation in that because Riley Conor was at least an equal to Guy Tavenner.

But no effete man of the East could strike Guy Tavenner. Especially when the man had been carrying on an illicit affair with Tavenner's wife. That fact seeped through Guy Tavenner's drunken brain as he reeled from the effects of Fell's blow . . . and groped for the revolver under his left armpit.

Susan saw the gun emerging and screamed, "Look out, Mr. Fell!"

Fell knew nothing of shoulder holsters. He stood his ground until the gun came into the clear. Then he cried out in sudden alarm and took a backward step.

Tavenner pulled the trigger. He was

almost stupefied with liquor, could not have hit a barn door at twenty paces. But James Fell stood only feet from him and Tavenner kept pulling the trigger until the gun was empty . . . kept pulling the trigger even after James Fell had fallen to the ground at his feet.

It was only a miracle that one of the wild bullets did not strike Susan Tavenner, who stood a few feet away, her hand frozen on the butt of the unloaded gun in her purse.

For a long moment, Tavenner stared at the man who lay at his feet. Then a shudder ran through him. For an instant he was almost sober. His eyes went to Susan, went past her toward Johnny Honsinger who was running toward him.

"Help!" Tavenner cried suddenly. "Help, they're gonna lynch me!"

The emptied gun clutched in his fist, he stumbled past Susan, toward Honsinger. The marshal drew his revolver as he came up and slammed the long barrel against the side of Tavenner's head. Tavenner went down like a poled steer.

Honsinger stepped over him, straddling Tavenner. He half turned, saw Tom Rosser come walking toward him.

"My prisoner," he snarled. "Don't you make a move."

"For him?" scoffed Rosser. He made a half circle to avoid coming within yards of Honsinger and Tavenner. He continued on to Susan, who still stood, petrified, before James Fell.

Rosser gave her a quick look and dropped to one knee. Carefully, he put a hand under Fell and turned him over on his back. Blood was oozing from the left side of Fell's chest. Rosser's eyes ran quickly over Fell, could find no other wounds and was surprised. At the short range, firing six times, Tavenner had struck Fell only once.

He said over his shoulder, "Get Doctor Kent!"

The command released Susan Tavenner. A shudder ran through her and then she came alive. She whirled, started running, past Honsinger and the unconscious Tavenner.

Others had seen the shooting, however. One had dashed into Dr. Kent's office and the doctor was coming out of his office as Susan rushed toward his office.

"Dr. Kent!" Susan cried. "Mr. Fell's been — "

He ran past her into the street.

35

SIM AKINS, wearing his new deputy marshal's badge, clumped up the stairs and went into the hotel. He found Moody behind the desk.

"It ain't true," he said to Moody. "Tavenner *wasn't* fired by Condor."

"Condor told you to tell that?" snapped Moody.

"Maybe he did and maybe he didn't," growled Akins. "And maybe it's just *me* who's telling you. Tavenner stays in jail. Don't you and your fancy friends try nothing."

"Get out!" snapped Moody. "And don't step back into this hotel until you're invited — by me . . . !"

Akins looked pointedly at the bandage about Moody's head. "You lost a chunk of your brains this morning. Use the rest, if there's any left, to think what's going to happen to you, you buck the boys again."

He pivoted on his heel and headed for the door, flinching as he went out because Tom Rosser stood on the veranda just outside the door, and he had to pass him again. Without looking at him.

Rosser intended otherwise.

"Akins," he said as the door swung open for the deputy.

Akins stopped.

"Turn in your tin star," Rosser continued. "That's *me* telling *you*!"

"I ain't afraid of you, Rosser," blustered Akins.

"Have you ever in your life had twenty-five hundred dollars?" Rosser asked mockingly. "All you've got to do is draw that gun of yours and put a single bullet into me. You do that and Riley Condor'll give you the twenty-five hundred. You're not afraid — you just said so . . . "

But Akins was already moving down the stairs.

It was ten minutes to twelve . . . almost four hours since James Fenimore Fell had been shot down on the street by the drunken Guy Tavenner. In the Pleasure Palace, Riley Condor was again haranguing members of the sporting syndicate.

"All right, I fired him," he declared. "He was on his own, but that's no good. The man he shot is James Fell. He's Mr. Big. Anyone else nobody'd raise a hand — after last night. But Jim Fell . . . Every man in this town is in awe of him. Every damn worker on that railroad swears by him. The vigilantes last night were nothing — a few scared rabbits. Now . . . isn't a man in the territory wouldn't join up with them. They hang one man — even an excuse of a man like Guy Tavenner — they'll continue to hang."

Not one of the men before Condor put up an argument. But Ken Rud asked, "We got to stop them from hanging this Tavenner?"

Condor nodded grimly. "If we have to kill off half the town!"

At five minutes to twelve, Wendell Lewis stepped out of his store. In one hand he gripped a revolver, in the other a coil of rope. He stood in the doorway and looked across the street. Mundt, the hardware man, appeared in his doorway. He had a revolver buckled about his waist and also carried a shotgun.

Feuer, the photographer, came out of his shop gripping a prewar Dragoon pistol.

Dr. Kent had salvaged the English shotgun from the dawn 'raid.' He was carrying it as he came out of his office.

Across the street, Josh Moody stepped out of the door of the hotel. He looked at Rosser, who still maintained the post that he had held so many long hours.

"I want you gone when we come back," he said soberly.

Rosser's eyes flicked up the street

and down the street. It was one minute to twelve. A heavy tramping of feet came from the direction of the railroad buildings. A solid phalanx of railroadmen were coming up the street. They, too, had been invited to participate.

Sight of them was the signal for the shopkeepers. Lewis came out of his doorway, started down the street. He joined Dr. Kent. Other shopkeepers were advancing. These were not the survivors of the dawn vigilante group. Oh, a few of them had been on that abortive expedition, but this new group of vigilantes consisted of virtually all of Great Plains, those citizens who were *not* members of the syndicate's ring.

They were converging upon the jail.

Sim Akins, who stood in the doorway of the jail, suddenly whirled inside and slammed the door.

Across the street, Rosser sighed wearily and went past Moody down the stairs.

Moody exclaimed, "Where do you

think you're going?"

"To finish the job I came here to do," Rosser said heavily.

He started up the street, passing the hardware store man, the photographer, three other vigilantes, moving in the opposite direction.

Rosser's destination was the Pleasure Palace, but he did not have to walk entirely up to it. When he was fifty feet away, men began to come out. Silently they formed a group outside the Pleasure Palace. They kept spewing out . . . a dozen . . . fifteen . . .

A similar group was pouring out of Ken Rud's saloon across the street, but Rosser did not even look in that direction.

Riley Condor and Johnny Honsinger came out of the saloon together, the last to emerge.

Rosser stopped thirty feet from them.

"Well, Riley," he said.

"Get down the street with your friends," Condor growled. "We're going to take care of them in a minute."

"No," said Rosser, shaking his head, "*this* is it for you and me . . . Right here . . . *now!*"

"Get out of the way," said Condor. "You haven't got a chance."

"Neither have you, Riley," Rosser said evenly. "I may fire only once — and that once with a bullet already in me, but you know that I'll kill you with that one shot."

"Hey!" cried Johnny Honsinger. "The old man's asking for a showdown, Condor — the twenty-five hundred still go?"

"It goes," grated Condor.

Sheriff Wes Parker came through the batwing doors of the Pleasure Palace. He walked sidewards so that he still faced Rosser, but was not too close to Condor and Honsinger.

"I'm sorry, Tom," he said, "but you told me this morning I couldn't run out. I had to play out the hand."

"I know, Wes," said Rosser. "You're Riley Condor's man. He brought you here."

"Worse," said Parker. "I'm also the man from Idaho . . . "

"Come on, old man," snarled Honsinger. "Let's start — "

Condor threw out his left hand, striking the edge of his palm against Honsinger's biceps. "Wait, you fool!" To Rosser he said, "His real name's Lee Ring. I paid him two thousand dollars to gun you in Kansas. He's the man who killed your woman . . . "

"I took the money," said Parker, nee Lee Ring. "I wish it could have been otherwise, but this is it . . . "

Honsinger could wait no longer. His right hand became a blur of motion. His hand shot down, whipped up his Frontier Model. Only the fact that Rosser was turned sidewards to him kept that first bullet from being the last one. As it was, the bullet burned across Rosser's chest, but did not cripple him.

Rosser did not even look at Honsinger. His entire attention was on Lee Ring. Rosser's best years were long gone, but this was the one time in his entire life that he *had* to be fast. And he was! He knew, even as his thumb whipped back the hammer of his revolver, that he had not drawn faster in all of his life.

He fired but once at Lee Ring. Then his gun was swiveling. "Now, Condor!" he roared.

Condor was going for his gun. He never got it out. Rosser's first bullet crashed through Condor's head, his second, for which he took time, slammed through Condor's chest.

Then Rosser was going down, knocked backwards by Johnny Honsinger's second bullet. The kill-crazy marshal was fast and could not be spotted two shots. His first had merely grazed Rosser, but his second was more accurately placed. It went through Rosser's arm, tore into his side and having been fired at a slight slant, lodged just under his right shoulder blade.

The force of the bullet knocked Rosser backwards so that Lee Ring's bullet barely grazed his thigh.

Ring was down on his knees then, raising his revolver for a second shot. But he could not fire it. Not at Rosser.

"Johnny!" he gasped.

Honsinger, his foe down before him, whirled on Ring. He saw Ring's gun swinging toward him and cried out in sudden fear. He triggered a shot from his gun . . . at the same instant that Ring's bullet caught him in the throat.

Honsinger was dead before he touched the ground.

Not one of the Condor henchmen, aside from Honsinger and the sheriff, had touched a gun. All had heard the dialogue before the action and knew that this was a private fight.

Rosser, on the ground, squirmed around, forced himself up to one knee. He dragged himself forward over the prone body of Johnny Honsinger. He shot a look at the face of Riley Condor, who lay on his back, his eyes wide open in death, and continued on to Lee Ring.

Ring lay on his side. Rosser's bullet would have killed him but Honsinger's also had gone into his body. He was still alive, but slipping fast.

Blood was gushing from his mouth. His eyes were bright as they met those of Rosser. "Another time, Tom . . . another world . . . "

Then the light went out of the eyes and Ring went limp.

"Another world, Lee," said Rosser.

36

THE pitched battle between augmented vigilantes and the syndicate did not take place. The syndicate was a Hydra-headed monster, but Riley Condor had been its central head. Its fangs had been Johnny Honsinger and — hidden — the sheriff.

All three were dead, and none of the other heads of the Syndicate saw any profit in fighting the vigilantes who now numbered virtually every gun-bearing male in and about Great Plains.

Nothing could be won by the fight except the death of the syndicate men themselves. They preferred surrender . . . and exile . . . which was granted them.

Prompt exile, leaving behind baggage, money and arms.

The exodus was going on even as

Rosser lay on his stomach on his bed in the hotel. His shirt had been stripped from his upper body and his hands gripped the bars in the iron bedstead while Dr. Kent probed and extracted the bullet from under his shoulder blade.

"All right," the doctor said finally as he let the bullet drop in the dishpan that stood on a chair beside the bed. "A little iodine now." He dabbed at the wound with the fiery stuff, but Rosser did not gasp. He had felt the shock of iodine on an open wound several times during his long career as a gunfighter.

Josh Moody came into the room as Kent was wrapping the bandages about Rosser.

"Fell just come to," he said. "He's swearing. Wants to get back to work."

Dr. Kent chuckled. "He's probably better off at work."

He knotted the ends of the bandage, reached under and turned Rosser over on his back. "*You'll* be all right, too. In about three weeks."

361

"Three weeks!" exclaimed Rosser.

"We'll feed you," said Moody. "And if you think you need a nurse, there's one up the hall."

"Mrs. Tavenner . . ."

"Uh-uh, her name ain't Tavenner, it seems. The tinhorn blabbed everything he'd ever done in his life. Seems he married a woman in New Orleans and never bothered to get a divorce from her. That makes his marriage to — to the young woman down the hall kind of un-legal."

"Josh," said Dr. Kent, "I've never wanted a snort so badly in all my life. Mind stepping down to your room and digging out that bottle you keep on your closet shelf?"

"Sure," said Moody. "Wouldn't mind a drink myself." He grinned at Rosser. "You?"

"No," replied Rosser. "All I want is some sleep."

Moody chuckled and went out of the room. Dr. Kent tossed his probe, a pair of scissors and a scalpel into his bag. "I'll look in on you around supper time."

He picked up his bag and left the room, leaving the door open. Rosser was not watching and did not notice that Dr. Kent had turned to the left instead of the right. A moment later, however, he heard heavy steps coming from the rear and rolling over slightly, saw Kent passing. Kent gave him a half salute.

"Went the wrong way."

More footsteps sounded in the corridor. Lighter footsteps.

Susan appeared in the doorway.

She looked at Rosser and he looked at her. A great weariness seeped through him, a peaceful weariness.

"It's over," Susan said. "All of it."

"All except the memories," said Rosser.

"You'll be busy," she went on. "You won't have time for memories. Except at night when you sit on your porch and look out over your ranch . . . "

"The ranch," said Rosser. "It never

was real. A home without a woman is no home at all."

"Perhaps there'll be another woman . . . "

He looked at her and a faint smile came over his lips. Yes, there *could* be another woman. It was in his eyes as he looked at her and it was in her eyes as she returned his look. Time . . . time was all that was needed.

And they had so much time.

THE END

FIGHTING RAMROD
Charles N. Heckelmann

Most men would have cut their losses, but Frazer counted the bullets in his guns and said he'd soak the range in blood before he'd give up another inch of what was his.

LONE GUN
Eric Allen

Smoke Blackbird had been away too long. The Lequires had seized the Blackbird farm, forcing the Indians and settlers off, and no one seemed willing to fight! He had to fight alone.

THE THIRD RIDER
Barry Cord

Mel Rawlins wasn't going to let anything stand in his way. His father was murdered, his two brothers gone. Now Mel rode for vengeance.

ARIZONA DRIFTERS
W. C. Tuttle

When drifting Dutton and Lonnie Steelman decide to become partners they find that they have a common enemy in the formidable Thurston brothers.

TOMBSTONE
Matt Braun

Wells Fargo paid Luke Starbuck to outgun the silver-thieving stagecoach gang at Tombstone. Before long Luke can see the only thing bearing fruit in this eldorado will be the gallows tree.

HIGH BORDER RIDERS
Lee Floren

Buckshot McKee and Tortilla Joe cut the trail of a border tough who was running Mexican beef into Texas. They stopped the smuggler in his tracks.

BRETT RANDALL, GAMBLER
E. B. Mann

Larry Day had the choice of running away from the law or of assuming a dead man's place. No matter what he decided he was bound to end up dead.

THE GUNSHARP
William R. Cox

The Eggerleys weren't very smart. They trained their sights on Will Carney and Arizona's biggest blood bath began.

THE DEPUTY OF SAN RIANO
Lawrence A. Keating and
Al. P. Nelson

When a man fell dead from his horse, Ed Grant was spotted riding away from the scene. The deputy sheriff rode out after him and came up against everything from gunfire to dynamite.

FARGO: MASSACRE RIVER
John Benteen

The ambushers up ahead had now blocked the road. Fargo's convoy was a jumble, a perfect target for the insurgents' weapons!

SUNDANCE: DEATH IN THE LAVA
John Benteen

The Modoc's captured the wagon train and its cargo of gold. But now the halfbreed they called Sundance was going after it . . .

HARSH RECKONING
Phil Ketchum

Five years of keeping himself alive in a brutal prison had made Brand tough and careless about who he gunned down . . .

FARGO: PANAMA GOLD
John Benteen

With foreign money behind him, Buckner was going to destroy the Panama Canal before it could be completed. Fargo's job was to stop Buckner.

FARGO: THE SHARPSHOOTERS
John Benteen

The Canfield clan, thirty strong were raising hell in Texas. Fargo was tough enough to hold his own against the whole clan.

PISTOL LAW
Paul Evan Lehman

Lance Jones came back to Mustang for just one thing — revenge! Revenge on the people who had him thrown in jail.

HELL RIDERS
Steve Mensing

Wade Walker's kid brother, Duane, was locked up in the Silver City jail facing a rope at dawn. Wade was a ruthless outlaw, but he was smart, and he had vowed to have his brother out of jail before morning!

DESERT OF THE DAMNED
Nelson Nye

The law was after him for the murder of a marshal — a murder he didn't commit. Breen was after him for revenge — and Breen wouldn't stop at anything . . . blackmail, a frameup . . . or murder.

DAY OF THE COMANCHEROS
Steven C. Lawrence

Their very name struck terror into men's hearts — the Comancheros, a savage army of cutthroats who swept across Texas, leaving behind a bloodstained trail of robbery and murder.

SUNDANCE: SILENT ENEMY
John Benteen

A lone crazed Cheyenne was on a personal war path. They needed to pit one man against one crazed Indian. That man was Sundance.

LASSITER
Jack Slade

Lassiter wasn't the kind of man to listen to reason. Cross him once and he'll hold a grudge for years to come — if he let you live that long.

LAST STAGE TO GOMORRAH
Barry Cord

Jeff Carter, tough ex-riverboat gambler, now had himself a horse ranch that kept him free from gunfights and card games. Until Sturvesant of Wells Fargo showed up.

McALLISTER
ON THE
COMANCHE CROSSING
Matt Chisholm

The Comanche, McAllister owes
them a life — and the trail is soaked
with the blood of the men who had
tried to outrun them before.

QUICK-TRIGGER COUNTRY
Clem Colt

Turkey Red hooked up with Curly
Bill Graham's outlaw crew. But
wholesale murder was out of Turk's
line, so when range war flared he
bucked the whole border gang
alone . . .

CAMPAIGNING
Jim Miller

Ambushed on the Santa Fe trail,
Sean Callahan is saved by two
Indian strangers. But there'll be
more lead and arrows flying before
the band join Kit Carson against the
Comanches.

GUNSLINGER'S RANGE
Jackson Cole

Three escaped convicts are out for revenge. They won't rest until they put a bullet through the head of the dirty snake who locked them behind bars.

RUSTLER'S TRAIL
Lee Floren

Jim Carlin knew he would have to stand up and fight because he had staked his claim right in the middle of Big Ike Outland's best grass.

THE TRUTH ABOUT
SNAKE RIDGE
Marshall Grover

The troubleshooters came to San Cristobal to help the needy. For Larry and Stretch the turmoil began with a brawl and then an ambush.

WOLF DOG RANGE
Lee Floren

Will Ardery would stop at nothing, unless something stopped him first — like a bullet from Pete Manly's gun.

DEVIL'S DINERO
Marshall Grover

Plagued by remorse, a rich old reprobate hired the Texas Trouble-shooters to deliver a fortune in greenbacks to each of his victims.

GUNS OF FURY
Ernest Haycox

Dane Starr, alias Dan Smith, wanted to close the door on his past and hang up his guns, but people wouldn't let him.

DONOVAN
Elmer Kelton

Donovan was supposed to be dead. Uncle Joe Vickers had fired off both barrels of a shotgun into the vicious outlaw's face as he was escaping from jail. Now Uncle Joe had been shot — in just the same way.

CODE OF THE GUN
Gordon D. Shirreffs

MacLean came riding home, with saddle tramp written all over him, but sewn in his shirt-lining was an Arizona Ranger's star.

GAMBLER'S GUN LUCK
Brett Austen

Gamblers seldom live long. Parker was a hell of a gambler. It was his life — or his death . . .

ORPHAN'S PREFERRED
Jim Miller

Sean Callahan answers the call of the Pony Express and fights Indians and outlaws to get the mail through.

DAY OF THE BUZZARD
T. V. Olsen

All Val Penmark cared about was getting the men who killed his wife.

THE MANHUNTER
Gordon D. Shirreffs

Lee Kershaw knew that every Rurale in the territory was on the lookout for him. But the offer of $5,000 in gold to find five small pieces of leather was too good to turn down.

RIFLES ON THE RANGE
Lee Floren

Doc Mike and the farmer stood there alone between Smith and Watson. There was this moment of stillness, and then the roar would start. And somebody would die . . .

HARTIGAN
Marshall Grover

Hartigan had come to Cornerstone to die. He chose the time and the place, and Main Street became a battlefield.

SUNDANCE: OVERKILL
John Benteen

When a wealthy banker's daughter was kidnapped by the Cheyenne, he offered Sundance $10,000 to rescue the girl.